Charon

Ian MacMillan

Published by

MELROSE BOOKS

An Imprint of Melrose Press Limited
St Thomas Place, Ely
Cambridgeshire
CB7 4GG, UK
www.melrosebooks.co.uk

FIRST EDITION

Cover by Melrose Books

ISBN 978-1-909757-69-1

Printed and bound in Great Britain by:
Short Run Press Limited,
25 Bittern Road, Sowton Industrial Estate
EXETER, Devon, EX2 7LW

MIX
Paper from
responsible sources
FSC® C014540

Cretan saying:

Stand still, Turk, while I reload.

Cretan mantinada:

> The tallest mountain in Crete,
>   Is called Psiloritis,
> And Freedom's eagle,
>   Has always there its lair.

Courage is the first of human qualities because it is the quality which guarantees all the others.
Winston Churchill

Dedication

This novel is dedicated:

– to my wife, Jean, and our four sons, Ross, Alan, Colin and Scott;

– to Lisa, Dimitri, Mo and Terry, who have provided such a great welcome to our holidays at New Kydonia, near Chania and taught us so much about the island, her history, and what happened during and after the German invasion;

– to the courage and determination of the Allied troops and to the unbelievable bravery of the Cretan resistance fighters and all those who supported them. They fought not for power, wealth, religion or dogma but just for freedom, for their love of their island, their home.

Contents

Chapter 1

It Begins

October 1941

The Kommandant stood, relaxed, at the edge of the old sandstone dock. He looked out over a velvet-black sea towards the harbour mouth. Around the edge of the harbour, the lights of the ancient town of Chania reflected in the dark Mediterranean waves. He threw the stub of his glowing cheroot into the gently lapping sea. As he started to turn towards the sentries clicking to attention at each side of the door to his headquarters, the hiss from his cigar extinguishing was matched by a different noise as the hunting arrow sped through the air to plunge deep into his left side of his chest.

Karl, the Kommandant's driver and bodyguard, whirled round at the sound of the thud to see his charge crumple backwards onto the jetty. He threw himself across the groaning body and screamed to the guards to fetch a medic and sound the alarm. The eerie wail of a klaxon was soon joined by others as the night cried a general alert. A squad of soldiers clattered down the steps. Some formed a protective cordon round their officer. Others dashed to shine their torches onto the water as Karl yelled out orders and pointed to where the attack had come from.

Two medics rushed down from the guard office closely followed by Feldwebel Brandt, the duty officer. The senior medic knelt and carefully examined the Kommandant. He winced as he saw the fast-spreading stain of dark blood welling through the uniform around the shaft of an arrow buried deep in the breast. '*Ambulance now!*' he shouted then reached forward. With a grimace of determination, and a firm grip, he started to pull the arrow out. It took all of his strength to slowly withdraw the well-embedded arrow. His companion pressed a thick swathe of bandage directly onto the wound and pressed it down firmly.

The ambulance raced through the streets of the town led by two motorcyclists, each with a screaming siren. It swerved into the courtyard of the military hospital where the waiting team of doctors and nurses grabbed the stretcher and rushed it into the emergency surgery theatre. Over two hours later Dr Erich Rafael, Surgeon Commander, emerged looking drawn and grey-faced. His medic's overalls were steeped with the blood of their Kommandant.

'Well, Surgeon Commander, how is he, will he make it?' asked Feldwebel Brandt anxiously. He stood at the front of the group of black-uniformed SchutzStaffel (SS) officers.

'Gentlemen, you have done well. Your Kommandant has lost a great deal of blood and the wound was deep. But he is a very fit man and because of the speed at which you and the medics responded to the attack, I am confident he will make a full recovery although it will be some time before he will be strong enough to return to his duties.'

More than one of the officers whispered a, Nazi unapproved, '*Gott sei Dank* (thank God).'

Back at the headquarters the operations room was a hive of furious activity. Officers barked out a stream of orders to their radio operators who sent messages out to the squads of soldiers hunting the assassin. Female secretaries placed red marker pins in the large-scale map of Chania as squad after squad reported back that another block had been searched and cleared.

On the floor above, a group of SS officers were carefully examining their only evidence – the bloodstained hunting arrow. It had been very carefully cut and ground into a perfectly straight shaft. One of the officers used a pair of surgical tweezers to carefully pick away the thin band of cloth tied tightly around the head of the feathered flight. As it came loose he saw writing on it.

'Gruppenführer, look at this. It is marked with a name, Charon, and has a sign next to it.'

The Gruppenführer examined the writing then turned sharply at the gasp of alarm from his deputy, who had been peering very closely at the arrow's metal head with a powerful magnifying glass.

'*Gott im Himmel!* (God in heaven!) A hole has been drilled in this, and it looks as if a wax has been used to seal in some liquid until the shaft struck. Radio the hospital now. Tell the surgeon in charge our leader may have been poisoned!'

The surgeon dashed into his patient's room and instructed the nurses to start emergency resuscitation. But he knew it was useless. It was obvious from the patient's cold, waxy skin that the deadly toxin had done its work.

Across the bay, by the entrance to the harbour, a black figure slid out of the sea and climbed up over the rubble of rocks that protected the foundations of the ancient lighthouse. The Venetians had built it during their long occupancy of Crete. In days gone by watchmen would keep a fire blazing in the cast iron brazier on its roof to signal the approach to Chania. Now a long shaft of white light from the searchlight on the platform high above the rocks probed the bay and the jetties.

The Wehrmacht (defence force) sentries did not think to look directly down below them to where the frogman removed a locking pin then pushed one of the sandstone blocks into the dark interior on greased rollers.

Charon climbed into his hideout, pushed the block back into place, removed the rollers and secured the stone again with the pin. He then pulled a thin plank of wood from a gap facing into the harbour and looked out at the increasing frenzy as the search for him mounted.

He slumped onto the cane bed, exhausted. Charon did not feel excited nor elated, just relieved that all the time he had spent preparing had been worthwhile. His campaign of vengeance had begun.

Eastern Mediterranean

Chapter 2

The Sniper

April 1941

Unterfeldwebel (Master Sergeant) Erich Weber felt omnipotent, yet insecure. Every sniper throughout history has to find a way of dealing with this feeling, which sets them apart from their fellow soldiers who would otherwise be comrades-in-arms. You sit like a Valkyrie in your chosen hide. You and you alone select who, when and how a soldier is to die. Your fellow soldiers look at you and feel closer to your targets than to yourself.

Many will have seen a fellow drop dead with an awful suddenness. Sometimes there is not even the crack of a shot amongst the cacophony of battle. No noise, no sign of a threat, yet a mate with whom they may have shared many years of campaigning lies, a crumpled corpse, at their feet. All of them know that a sniper can fire a great distance away compared with the range of their own weapons.

They can imagine themselves appearing in the circle of the telescopic sight pressed close against your eye. They may even shiver at the sense of cross-hairs traversing their body to heart or head and feel fingers nudging their own image into crystal-clear focus. Only those who have been shot and lucky enough to survive can truly imagine the stunning, numbing shock as your bullet impacts, before pain or oblivion. You walk solitarily and are feared.

You may be given a particular target, even a time of day, but you, and you alone, choose the exact time and moment to pull the fatal trigger, the slender lever between life and death.

Weber lay high up in an icy cleft above the peak of the Rupel pass, a key feature in the Greek army's defensive Metaxas line. He had squirmed forward from cover, his camouflage snowsuit blending perfectly with the mass of streaked snow and ice between two rocky peaks. He had watched almost dispassionately as wave after wave of mountain troops had attacked the old fort and had been thrown back. '*Mein Gott*, these Ancient Greeks knew a thing or two about defensive warfare.'

He wondered if this in fact might have been the actual pass which he learnt about in his youth. The scene brought back evocative memories of Classics lessons in his school in Westphalia about the Battle of Thermopylae, when a handful of Spartans had held a pass against invading hordes of Persians. They held the massed spearheads of Darius's well-trained troops for a long time before being defeated. A later Roman general, Pyrrhus, who suffered massive losses defending against hordes of enemies opposed to Rome's worldwide plan of conquest, said of his soldiers' success, 'Another victory like that will bring defeat,' so earning the expression named after him – a Pyrrhic victory.

The fort had been extremely well built. Massive blocks of sandstone had been carved from the cliffs by masons long ago then levered and rolled into place. It formed a semicircular wall at the top of a narrow, steep defile which on one side led north, into Jugoslavia from where the Germans attacked, the other led down into the heartland of Greece.

The thick walls formed a bastion around the gouge in the cliff from where they were quarried. The side facing the enemy to the north had an overlap with a narrow gap between. This was to allow one of the defenders to stand, safe from arrows, spears or slingshots, then to dart quickly forward, assess the progress and strength of the enemy and report back to where his soldiers sheltered.

Now, just as in those battles so long ago, the strength of the defences and bravery of the defenders meant that a mere handful, some thirty to forty men Erich estimated, had now held back the mighty Wehrmacht for four critical days. Though few in numbers they were very well equipped with weaponry, which they also kept replenishing from the crumpled mounds of invaders in front of them.

They also were very well stocked with provisions, enough to withstand a long siege, and a deep crack in the back of the quarry provided a stream of snow-melt from the mountain high above. They were clearly determined to fight to the death if necessary to prevent, or at least delay, the German forces' armoured columns trying to sweep down into their homeland.

So on this tiny piece of stony land the mighty German army was reduced to an old-fashioned slog of hand-to-hand fighting, man against man. The normal advance guard of the blitzkrieg, the squadrons of screaming Stukas then death-raining bombers, had proved completely useless. Because the mountain above overhung the fort and the pass itself was too constricted for manoeuvre.

It was almost as if the ancients had foreseen the day when airpower, artillery and mortars could attack down from above. The pass was also too narrow for the Panzer tanks, the mailed fist of the invaders, to clank their way through defences. Lines of sweating artillerymen had pulled their field guns up the rocky path, but their shells had proved ineffectual against the massive stone walls blocking their way.

Now the ground below the fort was littered with debris of

failure. Bodies lay sprawled under the dusty sun; some, badly wounded, crawled painfully back down to safety.

Each attack had been repulsed. The Greeks had fought like tigers. Bullets had streamed from narrow openings in the wall built for archers, now allowing excellent, secure fire slits. There was also a man-sized deeply slanted portal which allowed one soldier to stand and hurl grenade after grenade at the attackers, being replenished all the time by his fellows.

Now it was time for another form of attack. Erich had carefully studied the flow and ebb of battle. He had watched through his field glasses just brief glimpses of movement through the fire slits but could hear, even above the clatter of conflict, clear, confident commands from within the fort. Whoever was in charge of the defenders was very well trained and had directed the spirited resistance with great skill. Over the days Erich had added all of these glimpsed cameos together like a child painting in a numbered picture.

The commander of the defenders was a tall, dark-haired man whose dusty uniform was that of an officer in the Royal Greek Army. His second in command was a slim, short-haired, much younger man, similarly dark-headed. He was probably in his early twenties. Their tactics were that the commander would move to and fro across the thin line of soldiers barking commands that unleashed a deadly hail of fire in all directions. Then they would change soldiers when they fell back exhausted, and set sentries for quieter gaps between the skirmishes.

Should a sizeable group of attackers get too close for comfort or try to set up attack lines even using their dead comrades for cover, the commander would yell to the younger man who, with a small group, would dash in and out of the gap formed by the overlap, hurling hand grenades from a seemingly inexhaustible stock and break the attack.

But now it was the sniper's time. Erich Weber lay back to prepare himself, waiting for the next advance. He breathed slowly, steadily and relaxed his mind. He closed his eyes and let all the tension drain out of his body. A bugle sounded, followed by shouted calls in German to go forward. His right eye pressed gently against the narrow telescopic sight. One minute adjustment with his fingers and it was as if he was standing a few strides away from the entrance to the fort. Erich ignored the flickering figures, which briefly appeared at the window slits. He ignored the clatter of gunfire, the yelling, then screaming and just waited.

After a short time the attacking force was reduced to a huddle who bravely rushed forward towards the entrance.

The young defender leapt into sight, threw a clutch of grenades and turned back into the security of the wall. Erich sighted, aimed at the defender's upper right breast and gently squeezed the trigger. The heavy bullet ploughed deep into the young man and, as the sniper had intended, wheeled him round to fall face down half out of the entrance.

Weber reloaded so fast that the movement seemed seamless. Just as he had calculated, the head and shoulders of the commander appeared briefly in profile as he stretched out to pull the body back into safety.

A small adjustment and the leader's head appeared crystal clear against the cross-hairs. Once again the sharp crack of the Mauser M98K echoed across the gorge and signalled another death.

The sniper lay quietly, watching the dispirited defenders file slowly out of the back of the fort in retreat. He watched them leave through his scope. Again he felt this omnipotent power but enough, his job was well done. Only two shots, only two corpses, but they were the leaders, the inspirers, the heart had been taken out of the defence.

Erich Weber stood in the entrance to the fort looking down at the bodies, victims to his bullets, lines of mountain troops clattered by him as they moved on into Greece.

Many looked at him standing there so thoughtfully, then turned their eyes away from their own 'Angel of Death'. Some furtively crossed themselves while glancing round fearfully to check that no member of the SS saw their brief prayer.

Erich felt neither hate nor pity as he regarded the young victims. He hugely respected their bravery and the skill of the commander who had held off vastly superior forces for so long. Erich also admired the way he had thought nothing of offering his own life to save the younger man.

There seemed to be a familial resemblance between them. He searched both and removed their Greek Army identity cards. Ah, Nicolaos and Xanthos Petrakis, father and son, that explained the selfless courage. Erich picked up his rifle and made his way down the pass into Greece.

Chapter 3

Athens Hospital

April 1941

Senior Sister Brigitta Petrakis sat by the bedside table in the nurses' home. She desperately wanted to follow the advice of the head of the medical team to lie down, close her eyes, and fall into a well-earned sleep. But first she had to write to her son. Every week, since they had waved to Alexio as his ferry pulled away from Athens harbour heading for the safety of his grandfather Krios's house in Crete, she had written to him.

She had told of how bravely his father and brother had fought against the Italian troops who invaded from Albania. How that strutting poppycock Mussolini had boasted that he would ride his white charger through the capital of Greece, glorious as a Roman emperor of old, moving once again to make the Mediterranean the 'Mare Nostrum', an Italian sea. Mussolini envisaged his brave *soldati* crashing through the weak, unprepared Greek defences while in the North African deserts his armoured squadrons crushed the British 8th Army and advanced to Egypt.

On Mussolini's instructions, at 3 am on the 28th October 1940, Emanuelle Grazzi, the Italian minister in Athens, had

General Metaxas, the president of Greece, woken to receive an ultimatum.

Grazzi did not know the content, nor that Italian troops were already crossing the Greek border from Albania.

Metaxas gave a curt and clear response, '*Ochi*,' (no) to Grazzi. 'Ochi Day' is to the present time celebrated throughout Greece and her islands on each October the 28th.

Mussolini had not bargained for the bravery of the Cretan 5th Mountain Division who, in fierce winter warfare, crushed the Italian forces who fled back over the Albanian border. The Italian President, who saw himself as a new 'Emperor', had been advised by his military experts that twenty divisions were required rather than the ten under-prepared and poorly equipped divisions who crossed into Greece. Mussolini's response was, 'I shall send in my resignation as an Italian if anyone objects to our fighting the Greeks.'

Once again Hitler had been let down by his boastful ally, as was to be the case later in North Africa. Operation Barbarossa, plans for the invasion of Russia, had to be postponed while Germans troops were transported by train and plane down south to protect the Rumanian oilfields, the essential fuel source for the attack over the vast landscape of his enemy to the east.

First they had to invade Jugoslavia, after a coup supporting the Allies had swept the regent, Prince Paul, from power, before they attacked Greece. The German troops were a very different enemy to face than the Italians. They were highly skilled, battle-hardened soldiers. They had complete air supremacy and blitzkrieg rained down ahead of their advance. Although they were being held in the mountainous border region by the sheer bravery and determination of the Greek defenders, things did not augur well.

Even though Churchill had responded to his Greek ally's

plea for help and sent troops and planes from Egypt, it looked
as if it was too little too late to save Brigitta's adopted country.
Even now she had seen lorryloads of weary, dispirited, Allied
troops heading for evacuation ports at Corinth in the south, to
board again the warships that had brought them to Greece.

Now, rumours were sweeping through Athens that the
Germans had broken through the defensive lines and would
soon advance on the capital of this ancient cradle of human
freedom, the kind of democracy that Herr Hitler and his Nazis
seemed so determined to overthrow.

How she feared for her husband Nicolaos and Xanthos,
Alexio's elder brother. Both had been well trained as reserv-
ists. Nicolaos was an extremely popular leader, but against
the German armoured might and devastating air power what
chance did they have?

War had completely taken over all of their lives. Her mind
drifted back to happier times.

Brigitta as a young girl wanted to do nothing but become
a nurse. Even though, as a very attractive, blue-eyed, blonde-
haired German teenager, she was extremely popular, Brigitta
took little notice of the boys who clamoured for her attention.

She just wanted to become as skilled a nurse as her mother
and grandmother before her. Then her life changed out of
all recognition. She, of course, had heard her fellow trainees
gossiping about the handsome Greek surgeon, Nicolaos, who
had come from one of London's leading hospitals to take over
the surgical ward at Heidelberg Hospital in her home city. But
it was only when she at last gained promotion to become a
theatre sister in accident and emergency that she met him face
to face, well mask to mask anyway.

Brigitta remembered first noticing his gleaming, dark
brown, searching eyes, his tanned, lined face, and the mop of

shining-black, luxuriant, curly hair escaping from his surgical cap. She recalled first hearing the deep accented 'Thank you' as she passed sterilised surgical instruments to him and a mysterious tremor as their hands touched.

It was not long before he asked her out to dine with him. Their lightning romance was the talk of the hospital. In no time at all they were married and moved to take up a new life in Nicolaos's home town, Athens. Soon after moving to Greece their first child, a boy they named Xanthos, was born. Then, after some difficulties, their second son was born. Unfortunately, damage had been done to Brigitta's womb in the process of birth and she was advised not to have any more babies. So the daughter (who would inevitably have been so beautiful) had to remain just a dream. Perhaps Mother Nature after the horrific slaughter of World War I, in some strange way, was trying to keep life and hope alive with a new generation of males.

First Xanthos, then Alexio arrived on the scene. Both were dearly loved, handsome babies as dark-haired as their father. They grew up to be fine young men, the apples of their mother's eye. Xanthos decided early on to follow his parents' careers in medicine and train as a doctor. Alexio was still to decide his future.

Now her husband and eldest son were fighting a desperate rearguard struggle against their country's latest invader, high up in the mountains, whereas at least Alexio was safe in Crete with his grandparents. Brigitta took up her pen to start another line when the clang of the alarm bell meant she needed to rush to surgery as more shattered bodies were brought in for repair.

The Stuka dive-bomber swept in low over the Isthmus of Corinth. Its pilot could hardly believe his fortune. What a choice of targets. Queues of boats were embarking the long lines of retreating, weary Allied troops. The aeroplane banked its nose and dived steeply towards a destroyer overloaded with soldiers. Just as he reached for the bomb release, flak from a chattering anti-aircraft gun blasted into his plane.

The pilot pressed the bomb release button hard, but nothing happened. It took all his strength to pull out of the dive and wheel round. He could not understand why his seat felt wet, nor why his eyesight was becoming increasingly blurred. He pressed his hand against the sharp pain in his chest. His pilot's jacket was soaking. He looked down to see his lifeblood pumping away. His last, fading glimpse was of a large, white building looming up, directly in front of his windscreen.

The Stuka, fully laden with primed bombs, plunged deep into the side of the surgical theatre of Athens' main hospital, which collapsed after a massive explosion.

Brigitta just heard a crashing sound before her world ended. She knew nothing of the fate of her husband and eldest son; nor that Alexio was now all alone.

Chapter 4

Alexio Petrakis

May 1941

Alexio Petrakis looked out over the white-washed Cretan houses which lined the hillside leading up to the village of Galatas on its perch above the misty sea and the mainland in the north. His mind drifted away from the teacher's voice telling of the ancient gods and goddesses of Greece.

His teacher was halfway through one of the familiar Greek fables. How Athene and Poseidon competed for the honour of being the godparent to Athens, Athene's favourite city. A council of the gods had decided the victor would be whoever should offer the most welcome gift to man. Poseidon struck the earth with his trident and produced a horse. But Athene won by producing the olive, an emblem of peace treasured by Greeks.

Alexio was sixteen years old. Just one year older and he would have been with the fighters. Like many of the lads in the village, he had tried to enlist in the army now fighting hard in the mountains of northern Greece. But his grandfather, Krios, had seen how unsettled he was becoming as Alexio tossed and turned in his sleep, worrying for his family.

Krios was the unappointed but accepted leader of Galatas, sited high on a hillside to the west of Chania, the capital of Crete. Now an old man, he still had a strength greater than many of the youths. His olives were plump-full of oil. His goats in the mountain gave fine milk and cheese, and his skills as a huntsman had earned him huge respect. So when the recruiting agent for the Greek forces set up his stall to encourage the young men to enlist, it took only a quiet word from Krios for his young grandson to be turned away, dejected.

Krios was very proud of Alexio and at his age would also have wanted to fight for the defence of their homeland, but surely his son Nicolaos and Alexio's older brother Xanthos were enough for the Petrakis family to risk in this horrible war. And what of his daughter-in-law Brigitta, who was nursing in the hospital in Athens? Who knew how much danger could befall her when the German tanks and planes savagely attacked as they poured over the border up in the north, where Nicolaos and Xanthos were fighting valiantly against them.

Alexio thought about how quickly things had changed. One moment the whole of the island was celebrating the unbelievable bravery of their relations and friends in the 5th Cretan Mountain Division who first held back Mussolini's vainglorious Italian invaders from Albania. Then, with vicious hand-to-hand fighting, in terrible winter conditions high in the Pindus mountains, threw them back over the border in a shambolic retreat.

Just as the celebrations reached their zenith, the terrifying news came. Hitler had been forced to change his plans because of his Axis ally's inept performance. Again the German forces' meticulous military planning paid off. Speedily, lines of troop trains chugged south, laden with troops and armaments. Then, using the by now well-practised blitzkrieg tactics, Belgrade was bombed to a shattered ruin and the mighty Wehrmacht took over Jugoslavia in only a few days. Next they turned south-west and attacked Greece.

Alexio was completely oblivious to the two females watching him. His teacher, Lois, had noticed how the young man's mind had wandered again. How she felt for him, how she shared his pain and worry. Her husband, Abraxos, was also fighting the Germans, and she had heard nothing of, or from, him for months.

Almost all the young men had gone. Alexio was one of only three in the class who were either unfit to fight or had been stopped from leaving by their families. With a sigh Lois turned her attention back to her class and continued the ancient tale of Poseidon and Athene.

But one of her other pupils was also not paying attention. Melina was only fifteen years old but it was obvious she would be very beautiful. Her slim body was already showing the curves of the woman she would soon be. Like so many of her friends, her long hair was raven black. But it seemed to be shinier, to have a sun-kissed lustre, which attracted attention from all the young lads apart from Alexio. Since he came to their school from the mainland, he had never shown the slightest interest in her until she tripped in the road on her way home.

She had been so busy chatting to her girlfriends, including gossip about the handsome newcomer, that she stumbled on a stone and would have fallen in front of the old lorry if his two strong arms had not grabbed her to safety. How she had blushed as she stammered out a thank you, how her supposed friends had giggled at her embarrassment.

Now she watched him in thought so far away. She was of course aware of what he was thinking. She admired the fine features of his face, his dark black curls. She imagined being kissed by him. Melina knew that her love was young and new, but deep down within her, she was convinced that one day he would see and fall in love with her.

Alexio's thoughts turned to tomorrow. His *sakouli*, the Cretan knapsack of brightly coloured wool which his grandmother, Hestia, had made for him, was ready packed. The gun, a present from his father, was well oiled and loaded. His Cretan mountain bow was waxed and the sharpened arrows, each wrapped with sound-muffling cloth, safely secured in the quiver. Soon after he had bolted down the breakfast that his grandmother would insist he eat, off he would go to the mountains for another weekend's hunting with his grandfather Krios. Alexio would wear his hunting clothes. On his back would be tied his *panikryfto*, a camouflaged cloak.

Over the past year his grandfather had taken great care to teach him. First, how to shoot like a mountain man with gun or bow and arrow. Also, how to look after his weapons including, most importantly, his razor-sharp skinning knife. Then, how to stalk using the skills of a Cretan hunter. Moving with a slow, silent crawl, gently checking each patch of ground for twigs or stones that might slip, as the faintest of sounds would be enough to startle their prey.

He would slowly climb up onto the ridge and very slowly lift his head, covered by its black *sariki*, and inch forward, bringing the rifle slowly to bear. The ibis seemed to always sense danger. It would turn its graceful head and fix its sharp eyes, seemingly gazing straight at him. He would freeze, hardly breathing, until, relaxed, it would start grazing again. Alexio would then bring the gun up, so slowly to bear, it seemed motionless.

Then, moving his aim so that the sighting-pin in the notch was dead on its shoulder, he would take a quiet deep breath and gently squeeze the trigger. Krios marvelled as his grandson's skill grew to be expert with both the rifle and his Cretan hunting bow.

His grandfather would whoop in delight at another clean kill or groan in dismay as the creature ran off wounded. No matter how long it took, no matter how bad the weather, no matter how steep the slope, the two would trek on until the ibis died from its wounds, or stood, exhausted, looking at them for the finality of the killing shot.

That described how they would approach an ibis or group of them they had spotted through Krios's old, cracked field glasses. But at times the hunt was completely different; they would let their targets come to them. Krios knew these mountains better than the back of his hand. His father and grandfather had taught him his skills when he was much younger. He could predict, after a change in the weather, which tracks the ibis would use to seek water or shelter.

Well before the time they were expected, Krios and Alexio would select a good position, and then find a cave or more often a hollow in the grounds where they could lie concealed. Then it was time to use the technique invented so long ago and developed by their forefathers over the centuries. The *panikryfto* is a roll of old sailcloth, faded and battered from the winds of Crete.

The sailcloth was roughly torn into an oval shape large enough to completely conceal the hunter and his gun. The outside face of the cloth, when spread out, had been covered with a sticky paste of olive oil mixed with pine resin, both natural scents to the wild animals of the mountains. Placed face down on the dusty soil around the hide and pressed firmly on the ground, it would take on the appearance of the immediate landscape.

The hunter would then lie down flat in the hollow and pull the camouflage over him. Krios used to tell tales of hares, so oblivious of his presence, that they would hop onto its surface. Also he told of startling his fellow mountain men by leaping up in front of them like some demon coming out of the ground.

Alexio's grandfather had shown him many of the *kalderimi*, the donkey trails used since ancient times, the caves and cracks in the rugged terrain for concealment or shelter, the tracks the animals made and how to recognise each spoor. Also how to live off the land, how to light a smokeless fire using a flint and sticks, the berries, fruits and herbs to eat and those to avoid. Where, in the driest ravine, you could find water. Krios also taught Alexio how to catch and milk the goats which had escaped from the flocks and gone wild and wary high up in the peaks.

One evening, after a long hunt, they followed a hare that Krios had wounded, through some thorn bushes and into a cave no one knew was there. They spent that and many more nights in what was to become their secret den.

Alexio came to with a start. All around him his school friends were standing, gathering their satchels and going home.

The next morning, just as dawn appeared rose-pink against the horizon, Alexio was woken abruptly. Not from the gentle hand of his grandmother Hestia tugging him from his deep sleep, but from the crump, crump of bomb after bomb, the screaming wail of diving Stukas, yells and screams of alarm and terror from his people.

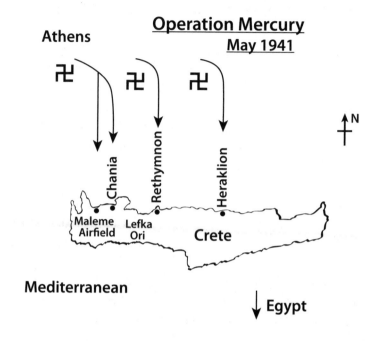

Chapter 5

Operation Mercury

20th May 1941
While Alexio had been sleeping the deep sleep of the innocent, the storm clouds of invasion were gathering on the airfields of southern Greece.

The German final orders for *Unternehmen Merkur*, Operation Mercury, the first ever invasion of a whole country, Crete, from the air in military history, had been given the go-ahead, but not without misgivings.

Hitler had watched with fury as his incompetent ally, the strutting, pompous Mussolini, tried to invade Greece in October 1940 without Hitler's knowledge, or, as many think, with his tacit but concealed approval. This did, however, prompt the Allies to send forces to garrison Crete.

The fierce resistance of the Greek defenders on their border with Albania, particularly from the Cretan 5th Mountain Division, stunned the ill-equipped, ill-prepared and poorly motivated Italians. Throughout the winter they were pushed back and back into Albania. Then, in March, when the Italians tried to launch a massive counter-attack, they were overwhelmingly routed.

Operation Barbarossa, the planned invasion of Russia, Hitler's major goal, had to be delayed by a month or so to allow the German forces to invade Greece to make up for the ineptness of his supposedly valiant ally, just as he also had to do in the North African deserts. Hitler's fear was that Greece, bolstered through treaty with Great Britain, could become a thorn in the flesh to the southern flank of Barbarossa. In particular, that RAF bombers might attack the oil refineries in Ploesti, Rumania, whose huge fuel supplies were essential for the vast distances the Third Reich's armoured regiments planned to travel.

So now, the plans proposed by his General Staff for a Mediterranean strategy were re-examined. These had been to neutralise British control of the Mediterranean through their powerful Royal Navy by the Nazi forces taking, first, Gibraltar then Malta, Cyprus and Crete thereby leaving the way open for ground forces to move to capture the Suez Canal, a vital link in the Allies' strategy.

But, when a cautious General Franco, not willing his Spain to be dragged into another conflict so soon after his Civil War, refused to allow German forces to cross his country from occupied France and attack Gibraltar, these plans were suspended.

Now Mussolini's inadequately equipped and trained troops had forced reconsideration.

One of the most enthusiastic proponents of these plans for the Mediterranean had been Major General Kurt Von Student, commanding officer of the *Fallschirmjaeger*, the German paratroop forces. Hitler had been hugely impressed at their successes on the Western Front in June 1940 and envisaged them as his own personal Valkyrie descending from the sky like avenging angels. This image appealed hugely to his supernatural leanings.

Operation Mercury planned a four-pronged attack over the day of Tuesday the 20th May 1941. After a sustained period of heavy bombing of the defenders' positions, parachute troops and gliders would make phased landings in order.

First on Chania itself at dawn, then on the three main airfields, at Maleme near Chania, then, in the afternoon, Rethymnon and Heraklion. After these were captured and strong defences established, troop planes and gliders loaded with hardened and highly experienced mountain troops would land and take over the fighting.

General Student and his staff expected to have control of all three airfields by the end of the first day. German intelligence told them that the defenders were lightly armed and in poor morale. As for the Greeks, well, they were almost disregarded. German troops were advised that they would be welcomed as liberators, a change from the oppressive Allies.

At dawn on that Tuesday morning the first lines of the 16,000 airborne troops involved, formed before their aircraft. The sun was just rising, pink over the Athenaeum, when the people of Athens were startled awake by the increasing roar as heavily loaded planes and gliders took off for the short one-hour flight to Crete.

The paratroops were in good spirits and believed with some justification that they were the very cream of Hitler's Nazi forces. Therefore they would have few problems securing the island of Crete and planned to take the whole island in three days. They would then reboard their planes and use the second chute they carried to invade Cyprus.

Nothing could have prepared them for the hell that awaited them. Not only had their intelligence staff hugely underestimated the numbers and morale of the defending Allied troops, they completely misjudged the reaction of the Cretan people.

Even worse, they were totally unaware that the commander of the Allied forces, Major General Bernard Freyberg, VC, from New Zealand, who had been in command of Crete for just three weeks, had direct access to the translations of the German military's radio traffic via top secret code breaking machines in England's Bletchley Park.

General Freyberg therefore knew the Germans' invasion plans as set out in Operation Mercury, both the timing and the locations they intended to attack. Sworn to the utmost secrecy, he kept this information to himself and did not even share it with his senior officers.

However, he too made a major mistake. Freyberg greatly overemphasised the risk of invasion from the sea, which anyway the Royal Navy took good care of. Also he had been forbidden by his superiors in Egypt to disable the three airfields, which could have been easily done, even if only that had been tried at Maleme. The Allies hoped they could be put to further use, for instance to attack the very oil refineries in Rumania which were Hitler's main concern.

And the second error, which was to prove crucial, was the lack of good radio equipment and an over-reliance on land telephones lines for communication. These were easily damaged by bombs.

Now we turn to another major factor in the invasion and its aftermath. The Battle for Crete in May 1941 was the first occasion in the war where the German forces encountered widespread and unrestrained resistance from a civilian population who then suffered hugely from their latest invaders.

In their Junkers JU52 transport planes and in gliders the paratroops had started off singing their favourite marching song:

We are few yet our blood is wild,
We dread neither foe nor death.
One thing we know,
For Germany in need, we care.
We fight, we win, we die.
To arms,
To arms,
There's no way back, no way back.

Then, when they approached their target, each retreated into his own thoughts, as harnesses were tightened and small arms checked.

And so the stage was set.

Chapter 6

Invasion

20th May 1941

Grandfather Krios was standing at the open door looking up at the flights of bombers and screaming Stukas as Alexio leapt out of bed and stumbled through to him.

'What's happening, Grandfather?'

'Ah, Alexio, it seems that the rumours we heard and dreaded about invasion are true. The planes have been bombing, strafing and dive-bombing the Allied positions relentlessly. I am sure they are trying to soften them up and terrorise them before they launch their attack.

'Now, without argument, I want you to load up our donkey, Meagan, with food, drink, bedding materials, firewood, your weapons and of course your *panikryfto*. Then make your way carefully up into our secret cave in the hills. When the battle is over I will come for you. If I do not return you must wait for one week then come back here to find your Grandmother Hestia and take her away to safety to Loules up in the mountains. There my good friend Andrea Padopolous's family will look after her and yourself.'

'No, Grandfather, that I will not do. I am sixteen years old and can fight as well as anyone in our village. I am now a man and will take my place fighting alongside you for my country. These Nazi swine have killed my father, my brother and, I fear, my mother as we have heard nothing from her since the Nazis invaded Greece. Do you really think I could live one more day with myself if I crept, like a coward, into a hole in the ground to hide, while you and your friends fight the invaders for our freedom? No!'

Krios was astounded that Alexio had defied him for the first time ever. Then, when he again thought back to himself at Alexio's age, a great feeling of pride intermingled with fear for the last of his line consumed his mind.

'Very well, Alexio, if your mind is made up you will fight alongside me, but for God's sake, no matter what happens, never tell Hestia that I agreed with you. Come now, we must go to the square.'

The open area in front of the tall Orthodox church was where the men of the area gathered at any time of crisis or when there was a new occasion to celebrate. Alexio and Krios joined the large group of men from Galatas and the surrounding farms then bent their heads to pray for victory with Father Mikarios.

All eyes then turned to Krios, their unelected but chosen leader.

'Men of Crete. The hour we have discussed so often has come. The German scum will soon attack our beloved homeland. Are you ready to fight?'

A loud grumble soon rose into a roar of agreement.

'We have talked many times about the best way we could help our Allied friends. This is to give them the advantage of our intimate knowledge of the land where the fighting will take place.

'Also your skills with the rifle, as long as you have not spent too much time in the *kafenion*, means we should all be able to bag a few of these fat Kraut birds as they drop in to meet us. Break up now into groups of about six and try, if you can, to have someone who speaks English, even if it is just a little in each group.'

Krios and Alexio ran down the square to where Lieutenant Roy Farran's two Matilda 2A tanks were sited. Krios had met, drank with him and had discussed how best to fight alongside his forces if the Germans invaded.

'Ah, Krios and Alexio. I was expecting you. It appears as if we are about to have some fun, eh?'

Alexio pointed up to the sky and yelled 'Look!' Lines of planes streamed over the area, discharging paratroopers who floated down to their land. Immediately a hail of rifle and machine gun fire exploded from the camouflaged trenches and the olive groves. Then ground artillery opened up, causing huge damage to the low flying transport planes and gliders. As the slowly falling troops, hanging on to their white parachutes, came down, many were picked off as if the defenders were shooting ducks. Next, as they came into land, some became tangled in the olive trees where they were easily killed by troops and by the hordes of civilians who came rushing from their work in the fields bearing the spades, scythes and axes they had been using.

The Germans were driven back after a long day of hard fighting but not before both sides had suffered heavy losses.

Later that night the *kafenion* in Galatas was full to overflowing. Many stood up and described their part in the fighting. The mood was serious but certainly not victorious. All agreed that the Germans had been brave, were very well armed and fought fiercely. They also had the huge advantage of complete air supremacy. Many of the Cretan fallen had been killed by strafing. Then a small group arrived from Daratsos where they had been told by New Zealand forces that the Germans may have retreated but had taken up strong positions behind Maleme airfield. The worst news was that the British defenders on the hill overlooking the airfield were withdrawing. Therefore the Cretans should expect to be attacked again, strongly, the next morning.

The following day Krios and Alexio took their rifles up into the bell chamber in the top of the village church. This was the best lookout position and for sniping the hated invaders. From here they watched as a fierce battle swept to and fro through their village. They saw Lieutenant Roy Farran's tank charge up the road firing its cannon until it was disabled by a German anti-tank rocket. They watched as fearsome New Zealand Maori soldiers attacked the German positions with incredible bravery. But it all proved to be of no avail.

By now the Germans had suspected that Maleme airfield was undefended and sent in a plane at dawn to check and confirm that it was safe. Then planeload after planeload of experienced, hardened mountain troops surged in and joined the attackers. Now the battle swung in the Germans' favour. Still fighting hard, the Allies retreated to the east, as a welcome darkness fell.

Krios and Alexio climbed wearily down from their tower and slowly made their way home through the carnage of battle.

After they had eaten and talked through the events of the day, Krios said, 'Now, Alexio, there will be no more arguing. You have fought like a young lion, I am very proud of you, but we have done our best. We will now go back out to where the fiercest fighting took place. There will be many weapons and ammunition. We will select the best and load up Meagan, our donkey, with them. Then you will now do as I ordered before. Go up to our cave and lie there for two days unless you hear from me. After that time come back here where Hestia will hide you for a while until it is safe.'

Reluctantly Alexio agreed and, as another dawn was nearing, he and Meagan the donkey reached the cave. He unloaded two paratroopers' containers and sackloads of their weapons, then, exhausted, slumped into a deep sleep.

Chapter 7

The Battle for Crete

May 1941

By this time the outcome of the battle for Crete had turned in the Germans' favour.

Their original plan had been to use the surprise and shock tactics that had proved so successful in Norway, on the Western Front and in overwhelming the Allied defenders at the Corinth Canal who tried to protect the retreat from Greece. So the military planners decided that they would attack four key locations on the northern coast of Crete. One to the west of Chania to capture the important Maleme airfield; another near Chania itself to attack the Allied forces' headquarters. Then, two slightly later attacks to capture the airfields at Rethymnon and Heraklion further to the east on the island's occupied north coast.

Their main problem was that the Allies were not taken by surprise as Freyberg knew their plans in great detail and had read the orders for Operation Mercury. So the defenders remained well hidden in the olive groves as fleet after fleet of bombers and screaming Stuka dive-bombers attacked their positions.

However, there were also three bad omens for the invaders as to the outcome:

#1 At 1 am, Major General Student was woken to be told by an alarmed officer that the British fleet had been sighted off Crete. Student coolly said that was no reason to disturb him or their plans and went back to sleep.

#2 The officers of the Storm regiment were told at their final briefing that the defenders were estimated to be roughly 8,000 strong, a quarter of the reality they faced.

#3 Part of the parachute division set off being towed by gliders. The glider carrying the commander of the invading forces, General Sussman, lost its towing plane when the cable snapped. He and all the members of his headquarters plummeted, like Icarus before them, to their deaths in the sea.

But the invasion was underway. When the gliders and transport planes began to offload their *Fallschirmjägers* (paratroopers) in the early morning around Chania, a deafening barrage of artillery and small gunfire broke out. Two of the paratroopers tactics proved to make them easy targets. Unlike the Allies' own paratroops later in the war they each only had one shroud. So they could not manoeuvre the direction of their descent. Therefore some drowned in a large reservoir, several groups dropped straight onto well-defended Allied positions and others onto farmland where the Cretan workers ran to attack them with their field tools.

Their other problem was that they dropped carrying only Schmeisser small arms. Their heavier guns, machine guns, sniper rifles, anti-tank guns, etc were dropped separately in marked containers. Many of them were shot as they dashed to retrieve the weapons and ammunition they so desperately needed.

The slaughter was terrible. In one company 112 out of 120 men killed. A battalion suffered 400 casualties out of 600 men. Planes and gliders were shot out of the sky. By the end of the third day German losses exceeded all those suffered in their war to date. However, the Germans fought fiercely and managed to take and reinforce two positions. One was to the west of Maleme airfield, the other was further south in Prison Valley where they made the prison their battle headquarters.

When news of the casualties began to filter back to Athens, General Kurt Student blanched, but he and his staff agreed there was no option but that the operation must continue as planned. Now the rush to push Mercury ahead so that Operation Barbarossa would not be too delayed, started to take its toll. The returning aeroplanes had to be fuelled by hand from jerrycans.

This, combined with the effects of the searing hot sun on the fuellers and armourers, meant that it was not until mid and late afternoon when the remaining attacks got underway. However, the delay had little effect on the eventual outcome even though the defences at both Rethymnon and Heraklion were as fierce as at Chania. Again the Germans suffered terrible losses, yet with some gains.

As night fell the time came for General Freyberg to take the initiative and launch a counter-attack at Maleme, as some of his officers wanted. But their commander was pre-occupied by the possibility of having to deal with a seaborne attack and marshalled his forces accordingly. Now the absence of effective communications proved crucial. The Allies had very few portable radios and relied heavily on telephone landlines, many of which had been damaged during the intensive bombing.

Freyberg did not know the invasion from the sea had been

well dealt with by the Royal Navy who, in spite of suffering major losses from the Luftwaffe, had sunk most of the caiques carrying the German troops. Further he was unaware that Hill 107, the key Allied position overlooking Maleme airfield, had been abandoned as his defenders withdrew after fierce fighting. The Allied forces did have fresh reinforcements ready to come forward but Freyberg delayed before eventually giving the orders. It then proved too little too late as the sun rose and his attackers were repulsed by flights of bombers and strafing fighter planes.

It became clear later that this was the pivotal point of the battle and, although the Allies fought on fiercely, the die had been cast against them and the end was just a matter of time.

That morning, having heard a rumour that Maleme might be able to be used, General Kurt Student had a plane from Athens land there. It was unopposed. Now the Germans switched all the focus of the attack onto Maleme. Hundreds of transport planes offloaded load after load of experienced mountain troops who rushed to join the attackers. Then heavy guns and transport flooded in.

By now the central battle was around the village of Galatas, some five miles to the west of Chania. The fighting swayed to and fro. Cemetery Hill, which overlooked the town, was taken, lost, retaken, until it became no-man's-land. The New Zealanders defending the area, particularly the Maori soldiers, fought with great bravery. But, eventually, the growing number of attackers proved just too much for them and they had to withdraw under cover of darkness.

General Wavell, the overall commander of the Allied forces in Egypt, was astounded to receive a telegram from Crete announcing that the battle was lost. Freyberg asked for the Navy to organise yet another seaborne retreat.

The defenders to the east around Heraklion and Rethymnon were similarly astonished to receive the order to prepare for evacuation. They had fought well and were convinced they had the measure of the Hun and could beat him.

Now line upon line of weary, dispirited troops made their way over the long track through the mountains to the south coast, to the bay of Sphakia. Here ships, escorted by the Royal Navy, began taking them aboard and on to Alexandria. In Egypt the Navy's Admiral Cunningham was determined not to let the army down. Officers expressed concern that their fleet might suffer damaging losses from German air attacks but Cunningham replied, 'It takes three years to build a ship; it takes three centuries to build a tradition.'

Eventually some 16,000 troops were evacuated to Egypt. On the 1st June some 5,000 Anzac and Greek troops surrendered. Some took their own lives as they had been in German prisoner of war camps in World War I and could not face imprisonment again. About 500 made their way into the hills where they were sheltered by the Cretan villagers. They then either joined the Andartes, the resistance fighters, or found some sort of boat and sailed to join their comrades in North Africa.

So the German forces were victorious. But later most agreed that it could very accurately be described as a Pyrrhic victory for the following reasons:

#1 The damaging effect that the Balkan campaign and Operation Mercury had on the plans for Operation Barbarossa. In Crete they suffered huge losses of some of their finest officers, troops, guns and equipment. Also they lost some 400 aircraft, mostly transport planes, which could have proved most useful in the forthcoming invasion of Russia.

#2 The Nazis suffered a huge shock to their morale from the terrible losses inflicted by lightly armed Greek and Allied troops and what seemed like the whole civilian population of Crete.

#3 From now on German intelligence was not trusted by the military forces to anywhere near the same extent as before.

#4 The subsequent fierce four-year resistance campaign tied up resources which could have been used in North Africa and Russia.

#5 The paratroopers were now grounded instead of being able to use their shock and awe tactics over the vast distances in Operation Barbarossa.

After Crete was successfully occupied, General Kurt Student held a crowded victory parade in Athens for his remaining *Fallschirmjaeger*. He spoke of their massive bravery and determination in the face of a much larger foe.

However, later Hitler saw Student one-to-one in Berlin and told him, 'The day of the paratrooper is over.'

Prime Minister Winston Churchill said, 'The spearhead of the German lance has been shattered.'

But now the villagers, who had hidden Allied soldiers, supported the resistance, and those who had attacked the invading forces were to pay dearly for their efforts.

Chapter 8

Reprisals and Vengeance

June 1941

It was eight days before the Germans returned to Galatas. During that time the Gestapo had worked hard to inflame the troops' desire for revenge. Many had seen the mutilated corpses of their companions as they buried them. They had been told that this was the work of the men, women, even children who had mercilessly attacked their comrades who had fallen wounded or who swung helplessly from their harnesses trapped below their parachutes caught in the trees. That the locals had brutally attacked them using any weapon they could find, scythes, daggers, spades and hoes which they had been using to work in their fields.

Only a few soldiers had noticed that most of the damage seemed to be bite marks and worked out that it was probably caused by the skinny village dogs that had been driven nearly insane by the terrifying din of war, the exploding bombs, the stutter of machine guns and the crash of grenades.

The paratroopers had formed the van of the advance against the determined resistance by the 5th New Zealand Brigade whose fierce Maori warriors' yells and courage had scared them so much. Both sides were by now well used to the sound of war. Each soldier was covered with dust and filth from explosions, each also reeked of cordite, the smell of war. They had slogged against each other to and fro until, exhausted, the Allies had been forced to retreat and they slipped away at night into the hills behind Chania.

The next morning the Germans advanced cautiously to find their enemy had gone. Their cooking fires were unlit; the only activity in the last hours of night had been caused by the small rearguard setting off a few flares from time to time to give the impression of action as their comrades trudged away.

Major General Freyberg, VC, the New Zealander who had just recently been appointed as commander of the Allied forces on the island, had decided that the battle was lost and that his forces should make the long march through the mountains to the south coast where the Royal Navy would evacuate as many as possible to join the troops in Egypt fighting Rommel. The men cursed as they had to leave their heavy arms behind to be captured.

The well-prepared, well-equipped reserve force could not believe the order to retreat. The soldiers were convinced they could give as good as they had been getting. They were quite correct in suspecting that one more determined push might have been enough to beat the exhausted paratroops and throw the invaders back into the sea.

But fresh German mountain troop reinforcements had now flooded into Maleme airfield and were ordered to pursue the fleeing regiments. The invading paratroopers had each been equipped with two parachutes. As they had expected, after a swift and easy victory on Crete, to be re-planed and next dropped onto Cyprus. Instead they had been ordered to take a much-needed rest in the camps established around Daratsos, Galatas and Prison Valley, but before that there was one further mission to complete.

The accompanying Gestapo officer had told the paratroops

that the local people from the villages had mutilated the bodies of their fallen comrades. The truth was that the packs of village dogs, driven nearly insane by the bombing and gunfire, had slunk back onto the battlefields at night. In peacetime they were skinny but adequately fed, now emaciated and starving, they were ravenous.

The night's battle noise fell away to be replaced by the normal rhythmic sound of the crickets chirring away. But now this was marred by the hellish sound of dogs growling as they tore at the corpses and the scurrying sound of rats.

Alexio and his grandfather Krios were hard at work replacing the red clay tiles on the damaged roof. Grandmother Hestia was going round the village, helping tend the wounded and trying to comfort the distraught new widows.

Krios lifted his head and peered at the plume of dust coming towards them. A jeep led a line of trucks laden with troops up from the main road to their village. Behind them clattered a tank.

'Quick, Alexio, down to the cellar. It is the young men they will be after, they won't bother about oldies like me!'

They pulled aside the kitchen table, rolled up the faded rug and lifted the trapdoor. Alexio climbed down into the stone cellar. Built as a cool storage area for the jars of olive oil, honey and rounds of goat cheese, these had also been used for ages as places to conceal women and children from enemies, or fugitives fleeing an oppressor.

'Alexio, you must hide in here. This is a private room known only to Hestia and myself. I tunnelled out this space with hammer and chisel, for an emergency just like this. There are candles, blankets, cheese, olives and water. Just pull this stone aside a little to let fresh air in. I fear all the young men may be at risk from the Germans but do not be scared, just wait here in safety until I come back to tell you that all is clear.

'Here is a gun I took from one of the swine. It is an automatic; its magazine contains ten bullets. Here is the safety catch, release it and cock it like this. If they should find you, don't wait a moment. Just come out fast, shooting. In the confusion you should be able to jump out of our bedroom window, which I will leave open, and escape into the hills. Go to our secret cave and wait. I will come and find you there when it is safe.'

Krios sat at the table nursing a cup of sweet, thick, black coffee. The door opened and Hestia entered. She was pale, trembling, looking older than her 73 years.

'What is happening, *kirissamou*?'

Krios could hear the clatter of weapons being armed and the thud of heavy boots marching on the familiar roads around their home. Voices barked out harsh, guttural commands in German.

He pictured only too clearly what was happening from the cries of his friends, their sons and daughters. He heard the women pleading for mercy as the Germans took the men hostage. His back door crashed open; it was his old friend, Mihalis.

'Quick, Krios, run and hide. You have been betrayed by that bastard Komminas, he has sold you out to the Krauts. Hurry, you must flee before—'

Mihalis fell forward into the room, blood bursting from his head as a stream of bullets chattered into him from a machine pistol. The front door was booted open and a massive figure in the hated uniform, face suffused bright red, raised his gun at the old man.

'*Nein*, Kurt, not yet,' barked a commanding voice, 'bring him to the square.'

The sergeant grabbed Hestia by the arm. 'You too will

come, old woman. You will see what happens to the cowards who slaughtered our men.'

A metallic voice from a loudhailer boomed out over the town. 'People of Galatas, you must all leave your homes now and assemble in front of the church. All of your houses will be searched. Anyone found hiding will be shot on the spot as a saboteur.'

Alexio heard the harsh commands but, remembering his grandfather's strict order to him, lay back, fearful as troops smashed through the houses.

Major Schreber of the 3rd Fallschirmjaeger battalion stood at the top of the steps to the tall white church. He watched as the villagers were lined up in front of him and one of his men set up the machine gun.

The square was crowded with women, held back from their husbands and sons by his fierce, war-grimed paratroopers. They glared at the women. Blunted by battle, still mourning their fallen friends, they looked with hate at the hostages, the filthy scum, for what they had done to them. Each pointed a fully armed carbine at the weeping mothers and daughters.

Another line of soldiers faced the men who were grouped in front of the church. Fingers nervously twitched against triggers as they hoped that some would try to flee the inevitability of their fate.

Major Schreber walked over to those to be shot and looked each one in the eye. Krios stepped forward. He spoke quietly to the officer in the heavily accented German he had learnt from his daughter-in-law.

'Sir, I can see you are a fighter. I believe you may be an honourable man. I am old, very old now. Please shoot me and the others of my age but let the young men go. They are but lads who have not even begun to grow the beard of a man.'

Tugging the wedding ring from his rheumatic finger, Krios thrust it into the Major's hand. 'Please accept this as a keepsake. When you look at it you will remember what you did today.'

Schreber turned and walked away, deep in thought. He stopped as the little, fat Nazi Gauleiter, Hartmann, strutted up to him in his black SS uniform. The Iron Cross, awarded for his courage in rounding up Jews on Kristallnacht, gleamed in the morning sunshine. His jackboots, polished by his orderly, shone like obsidian mirrors. He marched up to the Major.

'Heil Hitler, Major. You and your men have done well, I will take over now.'

Major Schreber, whose appearance was in dramatic contrast to this mannequin of evil, took a pace to the side and looked down at his dusty, battered paratroop boots.

Gauleiter Hartmann took out his pistol and banged the butt against the thick wooden door of the church. 'Bring him out now.'

Two soldiers appeared, dragging the bearded priest. The old women cried out as they saw how badly their priest, Father Mikarios, had been beaten. Dust and blood smeared his black robes and cassock. The men growled angrily.

'Will we shoot him now, Sir?'

'No, have him stand there. Let him watch what is to happen. Maybe then this man, supposedly a Christian, will spread the message throughout this accursed land about what will happen to terrorists, to all those who so brutally defiled the corpses of our brave Wehrmacht soldiers.'

Father Mikarios shouted out, 'No, you lie, it is not true it was the—' A rifle smashed into his side and he fell stunned onto the ground in front of his congregation.

Gauleiter Hartmann took the megaphone. His harsh voice,

heavily accented from his upbringing in the slums of Hamburg, crackled out over the square. To his right the schoolmistress, Lois, stood white and trembling as she translated to the frightened prisoners and their families. She had been told, in no uncertain terms, that her life depended on her translating accurately each word uttered.

'People of Galatas, and all the people of Crete. What you will see today you will remember for the rest of your miserable lives.

'What happens here will be spoken of throughout this island and send a message to anyone thinking they can resist our Führer's work to create a thousand-year-old Third Reich, and exterminate the world of vermin like I see gathered here before me. Heil Hitler!' he barked and his arm shot up stiffly, in a parody of the Aryan hero he saw himself to be.

He noticed that not one soldier had moved to copy him. No doubt they would use the excuse that they had to remain still holding their weapons, but their commander also stood motionless, staring down at the ground. Hartmann would not forget this insult.

Hartmann raised his arm, then let it fall and the clatter of the machine gun drowned out the cries of pain and screams of anguish. All the men fell followed by a deathly silence, only broken by the sound of sobbing women, as he walked through the pile of bodies with his pistol, giving a coup de grâce to any that moved.

The women began to move forward to their men as the priest rose unsteadily to give each a final blessing.

'No,' the Gauleiter barked. 'They will lie here, as our brave comrades did, for three nights. Then, and only then, can you take their worthless remains. Clear the square.'

The soldiers pushed the weeping women back at gunpoint

then set up a cordon, a grim vigil of death. Ravens, crows and the slinking, emaciated curs were the only creatures allowed to pass through the line of sentries, apart from the trails of ants and buzzing, black flies.

Hestia stumbled back down the hill leaning heavily on her sister's arm. As they neared her home she seemed to stagger, then clutched her left breast and collapsed lifeless in her front yard.

That evening, as the noise of the village died away, Alexio quietly made his way to the wooden ladder and up, to slowly push against where a thin gleam of candlelight silhouetted the trapdoor. Raising his gun, he tapped, then opened it. Hestia's sister, two other village women in mourning shawls and the priest had just started the wake for Krios and his wife. They leapt up, startled, as the black menacing figure emerged like some demon from the ground.

Alexio moved to stand over the two open coffins, carved in preparation some years ago by the Galatas carpenter. He stood looking gently down at his grandparents. His eyes filled with tears as he prayed for their souls.

Late that evening Alexio entered his church where Father Mikarios was praying for the souls of the dead.

'Father, I ask only one thing. Please find out where the traitor Komminas has gone. I have business to do with him. When you learn where the coward is hiding leave a note for me in your private place in the burial chapel.'

That night the black-clad figure moved to the cave in the hills where he brooded until the next morning, when he watched his beloved relations being carried to Cemetery Hill where they were buried side by side, together for eternity.

The white-walled graveyard stands on the hill between Daratsos and Galatas. The next night a shadow appeared by the raised gravestone, the burial place of the Petrakis family. Alexio opened the glass door and placed a bunch of Hestia's favourite wild flowers from the mountain inside, and then he added a jar of Krios's famous honey and a flask of his strong retsina.

Alexio went into the little chapel and lit a long, thin, yellow beeswax taper and placed it in the sand-filled chalice below the Icon of Jesu. After a brief prayer he opened the ragged curtain to the sacristy. On top of the pile of faded papers in the drawer where Father Mikarios used to make notes for the services, a piece of paper with his name on it said briefly, 'He is hiding in the barn at the back of his cousin's farm, may God protect and be with you, my son.'

Komminas woke nervously. What was the noise that had startled him, another of the rats nesting in the wall? Then a firm hand clasped tight across his mouth, the other held a razor-sharp knife to his throat.

'It is time, traitor. If you make one sound I will shoot you with this gun but not to end your life quickly. I shall take a long time to ensure your death is slow and very painful. Do you understand?'

Komminas nodded, his whole body shivered in harmony and dread. Alexio put the pile of gold coins in his pocket, which he would leave in the priest's offering box. At least the betrayal would pay something back to the people of Galatas. He led the traitor up the track to the centre of the village.

The next morning a small group of women from the village huddled by the church looking up at the body, swinging to and fro, in the noose dangling from the old olive tree. Alexio sat in the cave, planning his campaign of vengeance.

Chapter 9

Charon

Summer/Winter 1941

Alexio spent four days in the cave behind the thorn bushes, regaining his strength at the same time as he began to plan how to proceed.

It was strange taking the school jotter he had been using to note down fables about the early Greek heroes; now to write down his scattered thoughts then, after lying back on the mattress and thinking deeply, summarising:

1 HIDES
2 WEAPONS
3 APPEARANCE
4 NAME
5 PROPAGANDA
6 HELP FROM BRITS/RESISTANCE
7 PLAN FOR TARGETED, SCATTERED DEATHS

Alexio knew that his huge advantage was his extensive knowledge of the people, the land around Galatas and up into the Lefka Ori, the White Mountains of Crete. The disadvantage would be, particularly as Chania was the headquarters of the occupying German forces, that if all his actions were restricted to that area, their anti-resistance forces would be able to concentrate their efforts rather than wonder from where in hell the next attack was coming.

The Cretan resistance movement of fighters known as Andartes would create some chaos elsewhere. But knowing the history of his proud people, it was inevitable that their leaders, the Kapitäns, as in days gone by, would rise to prominence and vie with one another for fame and glory against the hated enemy. So his best plan was to wait until, hopefully, the British would send saboteurs, which they had promised as they retreated, who would help him with specialised equipment as well as receiving and giving intelligence on plans and targets.

He had two extremely reliable contacts in Chania. His Uncle Dimitrios, who ran the Aphrodite Restaurant and bar near the German barracks on the busy seafront. Also Andrea, his father's friend and soulmate, who just happened to be Melina's father, had a souvenir shop in Ritsou Street which was bound to be popular with the German soldiers looking for presents to take home. But in addition it was next door to a bombed ruin with an intact buried cellar which had an ancient smuggler's tunnel leading down into the harbour.

The other hides he chose, apart from the cave he and his grandfather had found when hunting, were in the base of the ancient lighthouse and the underwater cave by Aptera beach just along the coast from Chania.

Each hide would allow him to lie low for the two to four days it would take before the Germans gave up searching for him after one of his exploits against them. Every one would be equipped with a rough straw mattress or a hammock, flasks of water and wine, well-wrapped parcels of olive paste, hard wheat bread loaves and cheese, together with weapons, ammunition and costumes.

Every hide would also have a *panikryfto* available to use when approaching targets, as well as in some cases forming a temporary place of concealment. For example, on the dusty track south of Daratsos which leads up through Travonitus valley then into the Lefka Ori, there is a cleft above the gorge by the old wooden bridge which crosses it. This only fills with water during winter storms. Here he draped the oiled sailcloth over the opening, secured it in place by hammering in olive wood pegs, and tucked the bottom in secured with rocks. All it then required was a quick clamber up, pull out the bottom of the *panikryfto*, slide inside onto an old mattress then replace the stones, thereby securing it from view.

In Chania in the souvenir shop, Uncle Andrea was only too ready to help his friend's young son. They plastered up a door which had connected the two cellars, leaving only a small hole covered in by the top of a wine barrel. Over this they hung one of Mihalis's attractive Cretan rugs, woven in his shop only a few streets away.

Alexio kitted out the cellar with a German uniform from the dropped container, a sniper's rifle, pistols, ammunition and a frogman's suit. The latter, his father Nicolaos had bought him long ago, in happier times when Alexio and his brother Xanthos loved to go down into Elena Bay searching for octopus. During their times diving, the pair also found the entrance to an underwater cave near the beach which could prove useful as a temporary shelter.

It was Xanthos who had also discovered the secret room underneath the lighthouse which has stood for time immemorial, leading sailors to the safe sanctuary of Chania harbour.

The tale was that a stone tablet showing the Venetian lion had been secreted in this long-forgotten cellar. Now the Krauts had set up a lookout position and anti-aircraft guns where in times long gone by the watchmen would light large log fires on an iron brazier on the platform on top to guide boats into the safety of the sheltered bay.

The brothers had found that if they climbed up through the aged rocks piled around the base of the tower to protect its foundations from the fierce winter storms, there is an old wooden door which leads into the basement.

Alexio took the door away, then built up the opening with stone block work leaving just one access large enough to allow man-entry via a stone block which he levered onto well-greased wooden rollers.

That gave him two safe shelters in the capital of the island.

Alexio thought long and hard about what name would be important enough to terrify the Germans and impress his own countrymen and the Allies. Thinking back to the tales of the Classics, told so brilliantly by his school teacher Lois, he set his mind on Charon, appropriately the ferryman of death. Then for his symbol, he used an adaptation of the two-headed axe which Charon was supposed to have carried.

Over and above the weaponry he had taken from the battlefield, Alexio thought he would rely on the British fighters supporting the local resistance for any more specialised needs such as a sniper rifle and explosives.

Now, how to change his appearance so that he looked harmless to the Germans whose headquarters he decided to infiltrate? He was fluent in German from his mother and in English from his father. Both would be useful when listening in to conversations between the guards and their prisoners.

'You want me to do what?' Doctor Manossous glared as he shouted at Alexio.

He had been shocked at the change in Krios's grandson. Having carefully tended the scattered populations of the villages of Galatas and Daratsos, together with the farms and homesteads all around the nearby hillsides, there were few people and families he did not know well. But of all of them, the one who had gained more of the Doctor's respect than all the others was the Petrakis family.

Krios had been a very fine man with deeply held personal values and principles. He was extremely proud of his Cretan heritage. But he was also widely read and from his travels as a merchant seaman, all around the world, Krios had looked and learnt very carefully about different races, religions, their beliefs and life's ideals.

Although Doctor Manossous had retired more than six years ago, the villagers still called at his home for advice. Since his wife Siphi had died, these visits and reminders of the past had become even more welcome interruptions to the solitary life with his books.

Then the German paratroopers dropped from the sky to join the long list of those who chose to invade his native land.

Doctor Manossous was devastated when he heard, amongst the terrible news from Greece, of the death of Alexio's parents and his brother, then the terror of the German reprisals leading to the death of Alexio's grandparents, leaving the young man all alone in the world.

Now Alexio stood before him asking him to go against every human instinct that had developed through his long, dedicated life's work and training as a doctor whose role was to heal and save rather than to injure and hurt.

'Doctor Manossous, I have decided that my other life is at

an end. I will, from now until these hated Germans are driven from our shores, wage my own war against them. Alexio is now no more. My new name will be Charon, the ferryman of the dead. I intend to strike terror into the Nazi's hearts and destroy them, as they have done to my own family. But I have to be able to move freely amongst them. I will get a job in Chania, which will allow me to watch and listen to them. They will never know of my fluency in English and German, but if I still look like a healthy young man they would be suspicious and bound to ask why I was not in Greece or with the growing Cretan resistance.

'So the story I plan for them to believe, is that I was badly injured both physically and mentally during the invasion. But not by them, by a shell from the cannon of a British tank and that is why I supposedly hate them.

'I will act out the part of a simpleton with a drooping mouth helped by cheek pads, a vacant expression, but also with a severe limp. That is what I need you to help me with. I want you to create cuts and wounds in my leg which would look like the effects of shrapnel but only as deep as required for the damage to scar over without really affecting my mobility.'

'My God, Alexio—'

'Please, Doctor, not Alexio, Charon.'

'Right, Charon. I have seen so many torn limbs and shattered bodies recently that I would have no problem using my skills, but, apart from hating to disfigure your firm young body probably for ever, to allow the wounds to look realistic this will hurt like hell!'

'Please just do it, Doctor, dear friend of my grandfather.'

That winter Alexio, now Charon, got his Uncle Dimitrios to give him a part-time waiter's job in his Aphrodite Restaurant. The restaurant was at the very centre of Chania's busy seafront in the middle of crowded tavernas and eating places. It became very popular with the German soldiers who enjoyed watching the hustle and bustle as crowds passed by.

Some of the soldiers took a liking to this damaged young man, particularly when he told them of how a British tank shell had caused the damage to his body and how he hated them.

Charon soon felt confident enough to ask if there were any temporary positions for him in their headquarters. He explained that it would have to be temporary as he had a job in Aphrodite and in the summers he would have to go up to the mountains to tend to his aged aunt's herd of goats.

The Germans were delighted to help. It had been very difficult to find locals prepared to work for them and they were always suspicious of spies. But this mentally disabled young man would not be a problem because of his visceral hatred of the Allies for what they had done to him. They knew him as Antoni.

Charon quickly became a hard-working, indispensable member of their staff. Every day his knowledge increased of their plans, operations, informers and prisoners. It never occurred to them that this simple-minded youth might understand their language very well. He was soon passing highly valuable information back to the growing resistance movement.

Now it was time, Charon was ready.

Chapter 10

The Olive Grove

October 1941

Private Dieter Schultz was miserable. Why did it always have to be him to stand guard, bored?

He had thought when he volunteered to join the Wehrmacht four years ago that he would become a hero, respected by his fellow soldiers, and at long last put an end to the bullying he had suffered throughout his school days. He had envisaged himself as tall, bronzed, slim, fit, a classic Aryan warrior. His uniform pressed to razor-sharp creases. His athletic legs flicking up and down in a rhythmic goose step with his comrades. His head would swivel smoothly to the left as he smartly returned the salute of the inspecting general.

Instead it had just turned out to be more of the same old drudge. It was hardly his fault that his parents had both been small and dumpy with fat faces that drew cruel jokes from their fellow workers in the pork packing factory. It also was scarcely his fault that he had inherited his mother's poor eyesight which required him to wear thick, normally greasy, pebble-lensed spectacles.

The bullying recommenced in the army training camp.

The first day Feldwebel Brandt eventually got them lined them up. He stood, ramrod straight, twitching his immaculate, upturned, waxed Prussian moustache. Brandt glared at the shambles before him and fastened his monocled eye on Private Schultz, who stood quivering below him. 'Ach,' he barked, 'so once again they have sent me the finest examples of German manhood, the flower of Germany's youth stands before me in full bloom.' He poked Dieter's gut with his swagger stick through the ill-fitting, creased uniform jacket. It wobbled. '*Gott im Himmel*' he spat out as he left him to the tender mercies of his sergeants.

'Oh, what's the use of going over it all again?' Dieter looked over enviously at his platoon, supposedly his comrades. He watched them, all laughing as they played poker beneath an olive tree, probably the oldest in the area. It was gnarled and thick with leaves and early fruit. It gave the best shelter from the hot sun. Not one of them looked up at him, it was as if he just did not exist, they thought so little of him.

A flicker of movement down the track between the two villages caught his eye and distracted him from the deep well of self-pity he so often wallowed in these days. He looked carefully down the dusty track to Daratsos.

An old crone tottered down towards him. She was bent almost double under the weight of the huge bunch of branches, prunings from the olive trees, carried across her bent shoulders. Wisps of straggly grey hair hung down below the hood of her dirty, black dress.

Schultz stepped out into the road. He held his Schmeisser sub-machine gun smartly, diagonally against his chest. '*Halte!*' he yelled as she approached. It appeared she had not heard him as she came on towards him. '*Halte!*' he barked out his command again.

By this time he had attracted his fellow soldiers' attention. One called out, 'Well done, Schultzy, that's a real terrorist you've captured there!'

Dieter took no notice, as, angry now, he unshouldered his gun and started to turn it towards her.

He froze in amazement as the aged woman threw aside her load, ripped apart the front of her dress, grabbed the sub-machine gun strapped to her chest and sprayed a volley of bullets towards him. Dieter felt at first just a series of thuds, then searing pain as he collapsed lifeless. The merciless bullying he had suffered all his life was at last at an end.

His platoon jerked round and reached for their guns, but too late. A deadly hail of bullets chattered into them as Charon sprayed the gun from one side to the other then back again.

Soon all was again still and Charon walked over to his enemies. When he had finished arranging them he wrapped the old lady's robe, which had belonged to Hestia, around his waist, stuffed the grey wig in his pocket and moved away swiftly through the olive groves towards the foothills.

Major Heilmann started at the rattle of gunfire below the camp. He swore as his morning shaving routine was interrupted. He jumped, startled, and the open razor sliced a neat cut in his chin which began to drip with blood. His radio operator's response to the yelled query was that there was no response from the morning patrol. Heilmann issued a stream of orders as his men came running up, arms at the ready.

The jeep sped down the track leaving a cloud of yellow dust in its wake. The dust covered the truck laden with the watchful soldiers behind him. Major Heilmann yelled out '*Halte!*' when he saw the bundle of sticks scattered across the track. The jeep slewed to a halt, closely followed by the troops who dismounted.

They were greeted by the, only too familiar, smell of cordite and deathly silence.

No one answered their cries but sticks and leaves still

slowly drifted down in a glade where the bodies lay. The line of soldiers advanced slowly, watchfully towards them. Major Heilmann cursed when he realised the meaning of Charon's handiwork. Fat Schultz had been dragged to join his comrades. All the bodies had then been pulled into a very familiar shape, a grotesque pattern of death. The corpses now formed the double axe head of Charon.

Heilmann arranged his soldiers into a wide cordon around the new graveyard. Others were split into four patrols and sent out in the main compass directions to try to find the assassin, who they all knew would by now be well gone. As the Major moved to radio in a report about the latest of Charon's killings back to headquarters, his sergeant instructed his platoon. The soldiers moved over to their fallen comrades and began to lift them, to be carried back to the camp for a proper burial. As they raised the last corpse the sergeant suddenly noticed that a thin string had been concealed in the dust attached to its ankle.

It led up into the old olive tree, which overlooked the slaughter. His cry of alarm came too late. The tug removed the last part of the fuses of the potato masher stick grenades each soldier had carried. The pins had been carefully loosened until they were just ready to be pulled out. The bunch exploded and a merciless hail of metal fragments shattered the peace in the clearing and tore through the group of soldiers.

Major Heilmann strode, pale-faced, over to his shattered men. His grim, white-lipped mouth muttered a well-known oath about the ferryman of death.

Charon ran, as fast as one of the ibis he had hunted, to the dry gulch which divided two groves to the south. He clambered down its steep side and scrambled along to where it was crossed by a wooden bridge on the track above. He climbed up to its underside, removed some rocks from the side of the stone wall which were securing the cloth *panikryfto* he had carefully placed there, pulled it aside and crawled into his retreat.

Above him jeeps and lorries clattered across as he lay back quietly listening to the yelled commands as lines of troops searched for him. By night the noise of alarm had died away but he lay still, waiting for the following night before making his way back to the safety of his main base in the Lefka Ori.

Chapter 11

O' Tom and the Old Mill

February 1942

Lieutenant Colonel Tom Dunbabin of New Zealand was, from 1942, the senior Allied liaison officer with the growing Cretan resistance. He was known to the Greeks as O' Tom. He roared with laughter. God, it was good to be back in Crete. Kapitän Kyriakis had just told another improbable tale of his incredible bravery and cunning as he bamboozled the Krauts seeking him. What a bunch of boastful scoundrels they were. Yet, if he had to choose fighting companions in this rugged mountainous terrain, he could have chosen none better. How could the Germans have been so dumb as to not only expect little resistance to their invasion but also in believing their own propaganda that claimed the Cretan people would come to support them.

This from a nation who learnt how to handle guns from a very young age and who had been waging war against many occupiers of their beloved isle over the millennia. Also, if no invader was to hand, they would speedily start fighting amongst themselves. The men, dressed in the traditional clothes of mountain fighters, lay around the olive wood fire concealed in a cleft in the Lefka Ori. They drank raki and ate food brought to them willingly by the local villagers even though they had little enough to subsist on themselves.

But in true Cretan tradition the villagers would offer all they had to strangers to their land and in particular to the Andartes. They all had also heard the rumours about the tall Englishman and his radio operator who were fighting with the resistance and who the Germans were desperate to capture. The fighters, who all took great pride in their luxurious beards, were fascinated, if not envious, of the huge, bushy, ginger growth on Jamie the radio operator's face.

Now the scent of lamb kebabs marinated in wine and mountain herbs, which were sizzling on skewers over the fire, wafted over hungry faces. Platter after platter was handed round. Well, they had been travelling far over the peaks from last night's successful parachute drop of arms and ammo. It was time for a well-earned rest.

High above them their sentries took three-hour shifts as they watched for German spotter planes. They had little concern about attacks from troops on the ground. The group would soon receive a warning from any of the myriad of tiny hill villages.

Tom strolled away from the celebration, lay down quietly under an ancient oak tree and gazed at the stars twinkling through the leaves far above him. He leapt up at the sound of a thud into the tree trunk. Calling out an alarm he took a blazing branch from the fire and saw an arrow pierced deep into the wood above where he had been lying.

He unwrapped the cloth tied round its shaft. The message read:

Please do not be alarmed, if I had wished you harm I could easily have shot you. I am sorry to startle you, but this was the only way I could think of, to pass a message to you without being seen by your men. I call myself Charon. I am a Cretan patriot who has vowed a campaign of vengeance against the hated Krauts who are defiling our island. It was I who shot the Kommandant in Chania harbour. I am sure your sources will have told you things about that assassination which are not public knowledge.

For instance the arrow, like this one, was a Cretan hunting shaft. That one had a hole drilled into the metal head which was filled with the poison that killed the Kommandant. Also a small piece of cloth tied to the arrow bore my adopted name, Charon, who, as you know only too well from your studies of the Classics, was the ferryman of the dead, and a sign to represent the double axe head he carried.

I would like to meet you as we can help one another but it must be you alone. On the track that leads from Vamvakapoulu to Daratsos, just before that village, a bluff stands high above overlooking Chania and the coastline.

You will be aware that it is now garrisoned by the Germans' 95th Mountain Regiment commanded by Lieutenant Colonel Willmann. Below it, on the track, there is a very old ruin, an olive mill long since derelict. A dense Cyprus tree now grows up through its floor giving good shelter. I think it would be the perfect place to meet in secret. The Germans would never think of searching there, so close to their HQ. Their sentries concentrate on the approach road to the field camp. I seek information, advice on targeting and timings, and perhaps some specialised weaponry.

I will be there in one week's time, next Thursday night at 2.30 am. I know you will bring your bodyguards and carefully search the area to ensure it is safe for you. I will be watching and when they withdraw a distance, I will come to you.

If you want to change the timing or date of this meeting I suggest you leave a message in the shrine to St George on the corner of the *kalderimi* just further on, on the bend at the entrance to Daratsos village.

I look forward very much to meeting you, and promise that I will prove a very helpful addition to our joint efforts to removing these bastards from Crete.

Charon

At the appointed time, one week later, O' Tom sat on a stone slab amongst the rubble inside the ruin. His very suspicious guards, who still feared a German trap, surrounded the old olive mill. Tom had lit the candle stub and was reading the notes that had been left for him. They said, 'I thought it might be helpful and perhaps make you feel more at ease if I wrote about myself, what has happened to me and why I am fighting my solitary campaign.'

As Tom reread the sad tale and then put the papers down he was startled as a rope slithered down from the branches above him followed by a tall, slim young man dressed in black. Tom pointed his revolver at him.

The young man said, 'I understand your caution but you have will have no need of that. I am Charon and am very pleased to meet you at last. Also I have counted eleven of your men surrounding this building. They are all very well armed so if anyone should be fearful it should be myself.'

Tom relaxed, shook the hand the young man offered and the two got to know one another. He shook his head in wonder as Charon lifted the leg of his trousers to show him the fake bombing scars. He said, 'Charon, I am hugely impressed at your planning, bravery and the skill you showed in the assassination of the Kommandant in Chania. Why do you not come and join my group? You would receive a huge welcome and we could look after one another. You must live a very lonely life as things are just now.'

'No, O' Tom. This is my fight. I do not wish to be attached to any group. The Krauts would soon get to know of it and would redouble their efforts against you. Also they know who many of your men are, so would take and execute hostages from their villages. No, I must be solitary and completely independent. But that does carry a problem, which is why I seek your help.

'In six weeks' time, on the 20th April, Germans, all over the lands they have terrorised and occupied, will be celebrating the birthday of their Führer Adolf Hitler. I know about their plans for this special event in Crete.

'I plan to launch a campaign of terror between 7 and 11 pm that night. So they will never sleep easily in their beds until they leave my island. I want them to believe that there are a number of Charons.

'Therefore I want to organise attacks all over Crete and at each one leave this notice. I have written down my thoughts on how to achieve this, with separate missions from Elafonisi to Heraklion. I would appreciate you reading through my thoughts and would of course appreciate your own ideas.'

Tom read the plan carefully, then shook his head in amazement at the sheer daring, detailed planning, and thought Charon had put into his campaign of terror.

'My God, young man, this is marvellous. What an impact it will have on them, it will knock them sideways and how clever to plan it to take place at the time of Hitler's birthday.

My group and others will be proud to fight with you that night. Now I have a couple of other ideas. Let us discuss how I can help and how best to communicate and work together.'

The first glimmers of dawn reddened in the east as O' Tom and Charon went their separate ways.

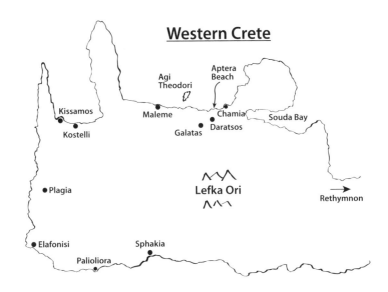

Western Crete

Chapter 12

Hitler's Birthday: The Officers' Mess

20th April 1942

Immaculately dressed stewards, clad in pristine white waiters' clothes, opened the swing doors and announced another group of officers clad in full dress uniform. Their blonde, closely cropped hair and glacial blue eyes stood out alarmingly against their white dinner suits, red cravats, and cummerbunds. They moved to mingle with their comrades-in-arms. Clinking glasses of vintage champagne, they discussed their time on Crete.

Just before 7.30 pm the stewards guided them from the cocktail bar into the dining room. Solid silver cutlery and crystal glasses gleamed and glinted in the light from the chandeliers. Each SS officer took his position behind his embossed nameplate, then snapped to attention as the main door opened and Hauptmann Hartmann marched in.

Hartmann, the head of the Gestapo, looked somewhat different to these tall, fit, perfect Aryan specimens of the Third Reich. But his small plump figure was hugely enhanced by his menacing black SS uniform with its silver lightning flashes and skull and crossbones. The Iron Cross with bars, awarded for his incredible courage and dedication in breaking windows and heads on Kristallnacht, stood proud on his chest.

Striding to the largest and highest seat at the head of the table, he barked, 'Today, the 20th of April, our victorious troops all over the fabulously growing Third Reich are celebrating our magnificent leader's fifty-third birthday.

'Heil Hitler, Happy Birthday, *mein Führer*, from all of us.'

The mess roared out their respects as stiff arms shot upwards and forward in the Nazi salute.

Hartmann announced, 'You may sit, *meine Herren*.'

Smartly the team of waiters served from tureens of lobster and caviar soup accompanied by bowls of warm pumpernickel bread. Hartmann commandeered the conversation with tales of previous celebrations of his beloved Führer's birth, his intimate and at times salacious gossip about figures high in the Nazi hierarchy. The officers, well aware of the power he had over their careers, attempted to make complimentary remarks and tried to ask obsequious questions.

The squid, scallop and langoustine fish course was followed with a plate of cheeses and cold smoked meats as an appetiser before the special main course they all were looking forward to. Just before it was to be served Hartmann rose to his feet and the room fell silent.

'Gentlemen, apart from celebrating the birthday of our esteemed leader, I would like to make further use of your company this evening. As I am sure you are aware, I have been sent here on the direct orders of Adolf Hitler to put a final end to the campaign of terror that has been waged in such a cowardly way against our brave troops.

'At the end of the meal, before we adjourn for coffee and cigars, I will ask each of you in turn, to stand and outline what specific measures you would propose we now take. I do not care if any ideas have been dismissed by other officers before; we need the benefit of your many years of fighting experience.'

Stomachs started to rumble uneasily and suddenly the focus strayed away from the main course to come. Three buglers fanfared the waiters carrying in a massive, whole suckling pig. Held high on their shoulders on a huge wooden platter, they marched round the table to cheers and appreciative applause. Just as they laid it down on the carving table the second in command of the Gestapo forces hurried in, bent and whispered in his boss's ear.

Cursing violently, Hartmann rose to his feet and said, 'Gentlemen, forgive me, I have urgent business to attend to. I am afraid that Charon has been creating hell again. Please enjoy your meal. I will be back with you as soon as I can.'

Hartmann was bending to enter his car when the head waiter cut deep into the pork and the bomb exploded. Later it seemed somewhat ironic that Charon's main target escaped his death because of the success of the spread-out attacks which had proceeded much faster and more successfully than he had ever dared hope.

Chapter 13

The Motorcyclist

The operations control room was a hive of increasing activity. Coloured pins on the large map of the island marked each reported attack and the location of the German troops.

Hartmann, the Gestapo chief, was in overall command. Still white with anger and fear from his near escape, his fat face was suffused with hatred and his eyes gleamed almost bright red as he cursed the name of Charon. It had already been reported that at every terror attack so far, a cloth bearing the same message was found as intended.

The bloodstained one that lay before him had been taken from the chest of one of the sentries guarding the main gate into Kolymbari. The Cretan throwing knife that had killed him lay beside it. The message read:

Nazi swine, your time has come. We are Charon. We are all Cretan patriots who have lost loved ones in your barbaric rape and slaughter of innocents in our beautiful island. Now, as you celebrate the birth of the evil scum who leads you, we are come in the night for vengeance.

We are not Palikari, nor Andartes, we belong to no group. We each have sworn a deadly oath to kill as many of you as we can until you flee from Kriti.

We each carry poison so that if taken we will gladly

give up our lives to protect the others. So there is no point you burning, raping, brutalising and executing more of our people, they know nothing about us and never will.

From now on you will not sleep easily in your beds as you will never know when Charon will come for you.

Hartmann called forward one of the waiting despatch riders.

'Take this order as fast as you can to Colonel Krakau of the 85th Mountain Regiment, stationed behind Mournies. It carries top secret emergency orders. Even if the officer is asleep, I want him roused immediately and leading his troops out at top speed. See to it or I will have your and his heads,' he screamed.

Similar messages were sent to the commanders of troops around Heraklion and Rethymnon and Kalymbari.

The orders read:

URGENT – To All Regional Commanders

A campaign of terror on this special evening which defiles our beloved Führer's birthday has been launched in the main towns along the north coast. You are to urgently take your troops, tanks and transport and establish road blocks on all roads, including tracks, leading out of Chania and the other main towns. You are to try and capture anyone who should try to break through but, if necessary, kill them. No Greek without a valid reason for being out after curfew is to be spared, man woman or child.

This has top priority. Deal with this immediately.

Hauptmann Hartmann
(Appointed by special order of Reichsführer Adolf Hitler)

Master Sergeant Karl Vogel wiped his dusty goggles with his leather gauntlets as he sped down the sandy track on the powerful BMW. He knew that his speed was reckless but his terror of Hartmann and a likely posting to the dreaded Eastern Front was much greater than the fear of a motorcycle accident.

Just as he headed into the final bend before the climb up the hill to the garrison he sensed a flicker of movement in the trees to his left. The wire tied tightly between two scrub pines on either side of the road sliced his head clean off, like a knife through butter.

The Andarte ran to the body, removed the orders from the message pouch on the German soldier's belt and replaced it with Charon's cloth. He then leapt onto the motorcycle and roared off into the mountains.

Chapter 14

Suda Bay

Captain Kostas sat alone, lonely, in the wheelhouse of his fishing boat, *Elpida*, which was named after his wife. His three sons had fought bravely as the Greek army threw the Italians back into Albania. Then the defenders were swept aside when the German armoured might swept across the borders. The news that all of them had been killed broke Kostas's heart. Shortly after, his dear wife *Elpida*, who had fallen completely silent at the dreadful news, just gave up her life and passed away.

He had pleaded with friends in the resistance to help him find a way of hitting back at the cursed invaders but was told he was too old. His reverie was interrupted by a hail from the jetty. Two large figures dressed in the clothes of Cretan mountain men addressed him in atrocious Greek.

They looked unusual and soon made clear that his suspicions were correct. They were saboteurs from the British Special Boat Services who had been supporting the resistance struggle. Over the moon to have such company, Kostas soon had them ensconced in the small eating area, below deck, out of sight.

First they introduced themselves, and by referring to the names of Andartes they had fought alongside with, and recounting acts of daring, ensured that Kostas was in no doubt they were who they said. The whole island knew that the hated Gestapo had tried over and over again to infiltrate the resistance movement by using impostors. Most were quickly found out and did not enjoy the end of their lives.

When it was clear that Captain Kostas was totally convinced, they said, 'Before we ask for your assistance, please explain why you are so keen to help in our struggle against the invaders.'

Kostas was dumbfounded when, after he had told the sad tale of his three sons and his wife, the one who had introduced himself as Stephen Verney said, 'Sir, Kostas, I am a minister in my real life back in England. May we say a short prayer for the terrible loss of your family?' All of them knelt and prayed.

The soldiers started to explain why they were there. But Kostas, tears still streaming from his eyes, said, 'No, not yet, gentlemen. Thank you from the bottom of my heart for your prayers. Now, this is my home. No Cretan ever discusses business without drink and good food!'

He served large glasses of raki then scurried off into the shops on the harbour front. He returned, laden with dishes of fish and shellfish, cheeses, olive breads and bottles of retsina. The three leant back replete.

'Now, gentlemen, tell me how I can help you.'

'We have a huge favour to ask you, Kostas. Would you be prepared to sacrifice your much-loved boat to damage the Germans? We would of course ensure you have more than enough money in compensation to buy a new one.'

'Gentlemen, your money is not important to me. Please consider my boat, and if necessary my life, to do with as you will. I have little left to live for.'

The soldiers explained that in two days' time, on the 20th April, the occasion of Hitler's birthday, a campaign of terror was to be launched against the occupying forces all across Crete. They worked late into the night, meticulously planning the attack.

At 8.48 pm on the evening of the 20th April, Bruno, one of the sentries on the German oil tanker *Ebarhelm*, which was fully laden with the fuel essential for the supply of Rommel's forces in North Africa, was watching the clamour breaking out in Chania, away to the west. He had heard explosions, then, even at this distance, could see and hear the sights and sounds of a general alert.

Too late, Bruno resumed the watch he was supposedly on, looking to the north and the Akrotiri peninsula. He screamed out a cry of warning as a fishing boat chugged out of the dark night, heading straight for the side of his ship. He did not see the rowing boat waiting and watching in the far distance as the three watched their attack.

The engine of the fishing boat had been locked at full throttle. The steering rudder was tied firmly in place to point the boat towards the oil tanker. With a deep thud it hit and the primed mines, detonators and explosives, packed tightly into the bow, exploded with a fearful boom. This was quickly followed by the gasoline in the holds igniting. The resulting explosion blew the tanker to bits and caused massive damage to two fellow ships and the dockside installation.

When patrol boats sped to the scene, looking hopelessly for any survivors, all they found was a lifebelt floating on the oily sea. It bore the name *Elpida* and tied tightly to it was a cloth, bearing the hated symbol.

Chapter 15

Rethymnon Airfield

Every evening a small transport plane lands at Rethymnon airport from Athens. It flies as regularly as clockwork, arriving at 8.30 pm with despatches from Military Headquarters in Athens, also transporting personnel returning from leave or replacements, then it leaves for the return journey exactly at 8.30 am each following morning.

Ober-Lieutenant Fritz Euller yawned as he saw the airport lights ahead of him. What a comedown for a skilled fighter pilot, but the splinter from the cockpit of his Messerschmitt Bf 109, blown off by a well-aimed burst of machine gun fire from the attacking Hurricane had blinded him in the left eye. He had been regretfully declared unfit for further fighter duties, hence this boring bus run.

Ach well, at least he was not fighting in the skies over Moscow where Stalin's defenders seemed to be putting up a much harder fight than expected and already the bitter frosts in the steppes were clogging the advancing forces.

As usual he flew over the runway to check all was clear then wheeled away out to sea descending, to loop back in and land.

From his many years of dog-fighting experience, he just noticed a burst of flame behind him. Fritz threw the joystick fast forward, but too late. The rocket barrelled into the rear of his plane, which exploded, then spiralled down into Rethymnon Bay.

The patrol cursed as they found the attacker's lair in a group of bushes behind the airport.

'One of our own Panzerfausts, the bastard!'

Then their officer unrolled the cloth tied round the shaft of the arrow and swore again as he read Charon's familiar message.

Chapter 16

The Souvenir Shop

At the far end of Ritsou Street, just before the narrow shop-lined street passes the ancient military barracks now commandeered by the Germans, it leads out on to the harbour. Andrea Papadopolous, known to all as Uncle Andrea, runs the souvenir shop which has been in his family for three generations. Andrea was an old man but still a giant. His girth would have crushed any donkey flat. His great, booming laugh was known to most of Chania, and his perfectly waxed, huge moustache was the envy of every Cretan male who met him. But one of the other things that strongly attracted the lonely German soldiers to wander around his shop had nothing to do with him but everything to do with his stunningly beautiful daughter, Melina.

Everyone knew that Uncle Andrea lived a complex and very full life. He would vanish off up to the hills to his family's farm to tend his goats and olive trees then bring their produce back to Chania. He also had been employed for years by the local authority in the town to clear away the mounds of rubbish from the bins early each morning and cart them up into the foothills to the landfill site. It was an astounding sight if you were up early to see Andrea at the reins of the heavily laden donkey cart, singing a mountain song at the top of his voice while the beautiful Melina sat, embarrassed as usual, alongside him.

However, only a very few people knew the other and much more important part of his life. He was born in Galatas. Krios, Charon's grandfather, was his lifelong friend and soulmate. They had hunted the elusive ibex together, wined, roared with laughter in the taverna and sung loudly of the bravery and heroism of the Cretan mountain fighters over the centuries of different occupations.

He regretted to the end of his days that he was not at his village when the scum assassinated his lifelong friend. Now he too had sworn a campaign of vengeance and was the only Cretan who Charon sought advice from and met with regularly to pass on the information he gleaned from the casual chat of the German soldiers, who were so dismissive of the locals that they assumed none of them could understand their language.

Corporals Dietrich Horst and Karl Willi left their companions singing in the fake *bierkellar*. There was just time to keep the appointment they had made with Uncle Andrea at his shop before they were on guard duty at 9.30 that evening. Each German ran fingers through their cropped hair, wishing to look their best in the hope that they might meet the shop owner's stunning daughter, the talk of their barracks.

Uncle Andrea looked up and portrayed a smile of welcome. He knew damn fine that they were not really interested in his display of Cretan souvenirs, old wine flagons, statuettes of classical heroes, paintings and rugs. Nor, usually of more interest to soldiers, an array of Cretan weapons, knives, bows with quivers of arrows and replicas of the swords carried by the Venetian pirates long ago. No, he noticed their eyes at once fastening on his daughter as she entered from the back room.

'Good evening, gentlemen, how may I be of service?'

Dietrich muttered to Karl in a supposed whisper, 'I'd rather have the daughter service me any day.'

As the Germans laughed, they failed to notice the fury that gleamed in Andrea's eyes. He barked, 'Melina, time to deliver those parcels to Cavalli's on Halidon Street.'

'Yes, Father.'

She left quickly. The soldiers were just about to follow her when Andrea said, 'Gentlemen, I have something new and very unusual that may be of interest to you.

As they turned he reached down beneath the cash desk and pulled out a stick grenade. With a flourish, he heaved the arming pin out as the Germans yelled '*Nein!*' and threw themselves to the floor. The spark from the flint lit the impregnated wick and the lighter flamed gently.

'Ach, a cigar lighter, *mein Gott*, you scared the life out of us.'

They agreed to repeat the trick in the dormitory as their colleagues changed shifts. Uncle Andrea then pointed out an interesting selection of replica German pistols. When the soldiers turned to have a look, Andrea brought out a further grenade and proceeded to wrap it carefully. Neither noticed the grim look of satisfaction on his face as they left his shop.

Once again sirens wailed as ambulances sped through the streets to the barracks.

Chapter 17

The Bridge

A sharp buzzing alarm woke the on-duty radio operator in the camp near Palioliora on the coast at the south-west of the island. As instructed, he went straight to the tent of his commander, Major Walther, woke him and accompanied the Major to the radio.

Hartmann outlined what had been happening all along the north coast.

'Major, we have to find these bastards. One of our inform-ants has just contacted me to say that a group of the saboteurs plan to escape by caique for Alexandria from the cove near Agia Keryaki which you and I have long suspected the terror-ists use. Please proceed there with your troops at utmost speed, surround the area and capture if you can, if not, kill the swine without mercy. I want a cordon so tight a rabbit could not get through.'

'*Ja mein Hauptmann*, it will be done.'

The previous night a group of local resistance fighters had laid their trap. Where the track along the very edge of the sea from Palioliora runs west, an old, but sound, wooden bridge crosses a deep ravine. The men had carefully removed all but two of the supporting beams and lashed explosives to them. Then they took it in turns to keep watch. The weakened bridge was easily strong enough to support occasional foot or donkey traffic. But one farmer, driving a shuddering lorry piled high with crates of fish, had to be turned back,

As timed, just before 10 pm, they saw the lights of the troop convoy approaching. Kapitän Leonidas waved the others back then knelt over the plunger. Leonidas waited until the Major's jeep followed by a fully laden troop lorry were halfway across then slammed down the detonator. The bridge, jeep and lorry crashed deep down onto the rocks at the bottom of the gorge. The soldiers stood no chance but the troops in the following lorry just managed to squeal to a halt where the bridge had been.

Unteroffizier (Sergeant) Gerhard peered over the edge. There was no hope of anyone surviving. They would wait until daylight for the terrible job of bringing the mangled bodies of their companions back up for a decent burial.

He untied the cloth draped over a branch, unfolded it and cursed his hatred.

Charon

Chapter 18

Maleme Airfield

Charon had saved this one for himself, after all this was where the invasion started.

Maleme airfield lies some ten miles along the coast, west of Chania. The airfield is narrow and long with runways running from the west to the east. At the back of the airfield to the west, a bridge crossed over the Travonitus river. Near there the Krauts had built a separate, but attached, double-fenced compound in which they stored all the ammunition, rockets and bombs.

It was sited a sufficient distance away from the control tower, maintenance hangers and air force staff quarters, so that any damage from an accidental explosion should be minimal. Yet it was positioned close enough for the armourers to wheel the bombs and ammunition to the waiting squadrons.

A high, barbed wire fence surrounded the compound. The only access was via an entrance gate into the rear of the runways. A watchtower stood guard on the corner by the main road opposite the store building, in front of which were the guard's quarters. Night and day the tower was manned and two sentries trudged round the outside of the fence, meeting in the middle to confirm that all was well.

Private Gerd Murrube took his duties extremely seriously. The youngest in his platoon, he bore all the sarcastic remarks with good humour as he was determined to be the finest example of German soldiery in his regiment. His uniform was as crisply pleated and pressed as was his sergeant major's. He did not walk on his sentry round but goose-stepped smartly on his well-worn route, while his eyes flickered attentively all around him. He was determined to go back to his village in Bavaria where he had always been regarded as a bit of a wimp, but to return as a decorated war hero. He was so busy picturing his triumphal entry with Brunhilda cheering him on, that he failed to hear the soft footfall behind him. A firm hand clasped his mouth, tilted his head back, and then a sharp pain in his throat extinguished his dreams and his life.

Charon quickly heaved him to the side of the path then took off the guard's uniform and cap, trying not to spread too much blood down the front. Mimicking Gerd's gait he marched round the fence to the halfway point.

Heinrich, the other sentry, approached. His marching was much more typical of a sentry bored out of his mind with another routine patrol. As they approached Heinrich said, 'Hello, Gerd, another quiet night, eh?'

He had almost no time to react as his supposed companion reached forward, grabbed the front of his uniform jacket, pulled him forward off his feet and neatly slit his throat.

High in the watchtower, Sergeant Kristof Becker nestled into the corner between the muzzle of the heavy machine gun and a corner post. His dozing ceased as a clatter came from outside the fence.

Becker started to turn the searchlight to investigate when a feathered shaft pierced deep into his chest.

Charon climbed up the wire fence then threw the coil of rope from around his waist, up and round a post. When the other end dropped down he tied both to the fence wire below the barbed wire then hoisted himself up into the watch tower.

He spent a few minutes checking that the training on the machine gun the British had given him was accurate. Removing two short ropes from his waist he tied first the searchlight, and then the machine gun, firmly into position. Both were aimed at the guards' quarters and therefore through them to the ammunition store.

Charon took a long, slow breath, then turned on the alarm siren and the searchlight. As the guards dashed out to be half-blinded by the light, the chatter of the heavy machine gun felled them like puppets, but the hail of lead continued until it cut through the heavy door to the ammunition. First bullets started to explode, next the boxes of ammunition. Then the first bomb exploded. This triggered the rest of the primed bombs which were on racks waiting to be loaded. A massive blast was caused which demolished the ammunition store and did severe damage to the control tower and aircraft hangers, even at such a distance.

Charon slid back down his rope and made his way up into the Travonitus gorge, to his cave and safety. But, just before he settled into a deep, well-earned sleep, he smiled wryly to himself and muttered, 'Happy Birthday, Herr Hitler.'

Chapter 19

Walnuts

April 1942

'Ayeeah,' Katerina groaned. Her back was really bad this morning. Perhaps the increasing heat from the sun, as it lanced and flickered through the leaves would give her some ease. How many times, she wondered, had she collected the pale yellow walnuts from this ancient tree. She stretched up and clattered her twisted walking stick against the branches. About a dozen wrinkled shells fell. She managed to catch most of them in her outspread apron. Enough now, she thought, any more and she would be likely to spill them. The ground around her was littered with twigs, oval green leaves from her work and a few nuts she had discarded as too ripe.

Her aching back was now really reminding her that she was an 83-year-old woman and not the agile, sloe-eyed young girl whose return had been so eagerly awaited long ago by the old folks when it was time to harvest the walnuts or the olives.

As Katerina slowly and unsteadily made her way down the dusty hillside path to the little village her mind wandered, as it seemed to do so often these days. Of Elias, the nymph, carved in ancient mosaics, dressed in long, flowing robes of gauze and always wearing her emblem, an olive sprig, in her long tresses. How she used to copy the goddess and was never seen outside without a similar frond or a bunch of the myriad of beautiful wild flowers which carpeted her hillsides placed in her raven-black, gleaming hair. Of days flirting with the youths and giggling with her girlfriends at the boys' bragging, boasting and inept flirting.

Then she thought of Nikoli in those far-off times, of making love with him. Ah, what a man he was then. His gleaming, perfect white teeth exposed in the grimace of his climax before he gently kissed her. Of how he always seemed to be smiling as he passed, waving to her on his way to work in the fields or going down to the coast to fish with his father. The smile that had made her decide, long before he had realised that he was in love with her, that Nikoli would be her man for life.

Her brown face, lined deeply by the sun, crinkled fondly as she imagined turning the corner and going down to the taverna below her. There he would be, as usual solving the world's problems with his cousin Gregorious. The two old men would be sitting at their usual table in the shade in front of their *kafenion*. They would each have a glass of ouzo, cloudy white from the few drops of water they always added from the other glass in front of them.

She knew she would receive warm, welcoming smiles and that they would praise the quantity and quality of her apron-load. Each would then select a few and with their strong fists, worn from many years of hard manual work, expertly crack them open against the wall and carefully pick the golden flesh from their sun-hardened, nutty wombs.

Katerina stopped again to gather breath for the last few paces. She turned at the sound of soft footsteps coming down through the trees above her. Whoever could this be? Almost all the menfolk had gone away to fight in Greece. Now many were dead, badly injured or prisoners.

Perhaps old Miki Akounmianakis had decided to leave his

beloved goats in the fold high up in the Lefka Ori and come down to slake his thirst. He was one of the very few who called now and his visits were as sparse as the hairs on his head.

Her smile, an embryo of welcome, changed to surprise as the footsteps grew louder and a young man, tall, slim and dressed in the clothes of a Cretan mountaineer, emerged onto the path. She gasped as she saw what he was shouldering.

Not one of the old embossed guns so beloved by the shepherds, nor one of the British rifles left behind as they retreated, which the partisans used, but the kind of carbine carried by the Germans who, weary from another fruitless search, high on the dry mountainsides, would stagger out of their Kubbelwagons and seek a drink in the café.

'Mother, *kali mera*,' the young man said, smiling to put her at her ease, noticing and understanding her concern and fear over his unexpected appearance.

'*Mera*, my son. You startled me. We do not see many strangers here. Where have you come from?'

'I have been visiting my Aunt Eleni in Loussakies and decided to come back across the mountains rather than risk meeting the accursed Germans out on their patrols.'

'Where did you get that gun from, my son?'

'From one of the three swine that I killed a few days ago. It was with great luck that I happened to come across them as they were trying to steal chickens from a young woman. Heaven alone knows what fate might have befallen her if I had not chanced by.'

'What a curse they are to our beautiful island. It makes my old heart weep when I hear another tale of their savagery. You must come down to our *kafenion* in Perivolia. My husband Nikoli and Gregorious, his cousin, will be eager to hear your news, will want to meet you and drink to your bravery. Also you must be tired after your long walk. You will stay over and eat with us and rest. We do not often have guests these days; it would be a very good thing and make us happy if you would stay at our home.

'Perhaps you would also like to join us at our church tomorrow, Easter Sunday, as we remember Jesus's sacrifice for us? It is also our patron Saint Gerasimos's day. We could all pray to God that the Germans would leave.'

Charon laughed in delight at the kindliness expressed in the hospitality offered so readily by the old lady, so typical of his fellow Cretans and willingly accepted.

That night Nikoli and Gregorious clapped their hands on the table in pleasure as the young man regaled them with stories of terror, horror, daring and adventure.

The two old men felt the sap rising again, the old familiar tingle of excitement stirring their worn but tough sinews with passion, the sauce of their distant youth. They stroked their long, drooping, once dark moustaches, now stained from ouzo, retsina and Katerina's fine cooking, as they peered through veined eyes and listened hard through fading ears to the tales from Charon.

'This is a very fine weapon, my friend. You will kill many of the beasts with this and avenge the death of so many of our people.'

The next day was Easter Sunday. This is probably the most important religious festival in Greece and her islands. The old couple were delighted when Charon asked if he could come to the service in their local church. Charon climbed up on the back of the cart. Nikoli tugged the reins and the aged donkeys pulled them slowly up the twisty track towards the hollow clanking of the church bells as they called out in supplication over the village. Katerina explained to the village priest who the young man was as he knelt quietly before the table with the wooden cross flanked by two tall, yellow beeswax candles.

Charon thanked Saint Gerasimos for the kindness and warmth of his welcome. He prayed again to the memory of his brother, parents, grandfather, grandmother and all those who had fallen. Then Charon prayed to God to support him, to be with him and to give him the strength to never stop in his search for vengeance.

Towards the end of the service, the priest lit a single, sacred candle and cried out, '*Christos Anesti!*' (Christ is risen!). He touched his taper to another held by one of his fellow priests who did the same to the person next to him and so the blessing continued. Soon the whole church was glowing with the soft light from prayer candles and the shouts of '*Christos Anesti!*' rose to the roof as families embraced and hugged one another.

After the service, the congregation filed out and the priest led them in a long line, chanting blessings, three times round the church. Then each family tore a sprig from the very old gnarled olive tree which the reverend father blessed. The olive branch was then taken back home as a good luck charm to protect their families over the coming year. It was now the time for each family to open their long-saved provisions and feast in celebration.

When Charon departed from the old couple, both entreated him to think of their home as his own and that if he ever needed a safe hiding place not to hesitate but come back to them.

Chapter 20

Heraklion Airfield

May 1942

Just after midnight a dark figure crossed the track to the wayside shrine. Charon gently lifted the statuette of Saint Michael and removed the neatly folded piece of paper concealed beneath it. All it said was, 'Thursday 11 pm, usual place'.

Early the next Saturday morning he sat waiting in the ruin, as agreed previously, two days later and three hours after the time stated in the message. A soft shuffle of feet outside signalled the arrival of Tom Dunbabin and his bodyguards.

Tom came in and embraced Charon, kissing each other on each cheek as Greeks have done for centuries.

'Charon, your plan worked brilliantly. The Krauts are going bananas trying to work out who you are and have fallen completely for your idea that there are a number of you operating under the name Charon all across Crete. Their soldiers are increasingly terrified of the dark.

'I now need your help for an extremely secret and important mission, which could have a major effect on the war in North Africa.

'You may have heard that Rommel's forces in Libya surround our troops in Tobruk. We are desperately short of supplies and a fleet is sailing in four days' time from our base in Malta to bring vitally needed supplies of fuel, ammo and food.

'Now, this is the most important wartime secret I will ever entrust you to keep. We have captured an Enigma coding machine and can read all the Germans' military messages.

'Through this we have learnt that a spy in Egypt has informed Nazi intelligence of the plans for the relief convoy. They are therefore sending four flights of bombers to Heraklion airfield; they will be there tomorrow. The following Tuesday, at dawn, they plan to completely destroy our fleet as it approaches Tobruk.

'We have to stop them. I have therefore arranged for two expert saboteurs from the Special Boat Service to be landed by submarine on the coast near to Heraklion. You know the Stavros lighthouse? Well, we have learnt that the bay next to it, Orrnos Alikis, is not guarded by the Boche so it should be a safe place to land.

'We have arranged that Father Ikanos of Agia Pelagia will look after you, then the next evening you make your way to Heraklion airport, it's only about a two-hour hike. You can reconnoitre the airfield the next day ready to sabotage the bombers who will be fully loaded, armed up and ready to fly early the next morning.

'I want you to meet the saboteurs in the early hours at the bay in about twenty-four hours' time.

'The submarine will surface at around 3 am and watch for your torch signal of three short flashes then one long. If you could repeat this every three hours, I hope you will see the reply of one short flash and two long.

'As you understand only too well, we will be relying on you to keep a very careful watch for any German patrols.

'You will then act as the guide to the hide you chose last year overlooking the airfield. Lie up there, watching all that's going on during Monday, then attack early on the Tuesday morning.

'Just before you begin, two of our bombers from Egypt will

hit the control tower at Heraklion to create enough havoc and confusion to allow you and the SBS (Special Boat Section) chaps to plant timed limpet mines in the bomb bays of the planes, which we expect will be left unguarded during the diversionary raid.'

'My friend, I can think of nothing better to do over the next few days than to blow German planes out of the sky! Now I need to get moving so I can catch the early morning bus along the coast from Chania.'

Sandy and Lofty looked the most unlikely pair of military experts. But, like many great partnerships their complementary strengths made the couple a very powerful force to be reckoned with. Sandy MacBain was almost a perfect caricature of a massive, freckled, redheaded, belligerent Glaswegian. It was as if he had been born with a point to prove. His quick anger got him into all sorts of trouble from a very early age. He was in and out of foster homes, borstal then prison. His father, an ex-service man, was delighted when at last Sandy took some advice from him and joined up in the army.

He excelled throughout his training with the Highland Light Infantry and was soon spotted by officers seeking men of a special nature to obey Churchill's diktat to set Europe ablaze.

Lofty of course was nicknamed with typical army humour. He was tiny, just five feet one inch in his stockings. He looked like a pygmy beside the giant muscular figure of his comrade in arms Sandy.

But Lofty had been recruited, not for his military prowess, but because he was known throughout his native Wales as an expert with explosives. He worked for a demolition contractor. Lofty, after a brief survey, could tell exactly how much of what kind of explosive should be used and exactly where it should be placed

Now, for a man whose only known fear was claustrophobia, he literally quivered with terror as the German depth charges exploded around their submarine from the Royal Navy base in Alexandria as it approached the coast of Crete.

They waited for two hours on the seabed until the planes gave up their attack. The submarine slid slowly to the surface. Dimitri, the bearded, extrovert captain of the Greek submarine *Triton*, looked exactly like a buccaneer from the past. He raised the slim periscope and scanned the surface of the bay.

'OK, gentlemen, all clear, looks as if the bastards have given up on us. We'll now move in closer to the shore and watch for the signal we expect from your guide.'

The sub swayed gently in the swell as Captain Dimitri scanned the dark, approaching coastline through his binoculars. 'There!' he shouted to his No. 2 as he saw three short blinks of torchlight then a long flash. He signalled the agreed reply.

Sandy and Lofty slid easily into the bobbing rubber dinghy. The sailors then gingerly handed down their rucksacks, heavy with mines and detonators. The captain said, 'We will wait around here watching for your signal over the next three nights. Good luck, lads, give those bastards hell.' Captain Dimitri saluted as Lofty and Sandy rowed away towards the dark coast.

Neither of the saboteurs spoke as they grounded in the shallows and stepped out, half-expecting a hail of machine gun bullets to rip them apart. But it was not to be. A dark figure emerged from the gloom and in fluent English said, 'Welcome to my beloved Crete, my friends; I am Charon, your guide.'

It was only a short hike to the little white church on the rise above the sleeping village of Agia Pelagia. Sandy and Lofty soon regained their land legs and enjoyed deeply breathing in the mild, thyme-scented night air, a delight after the stuffy atmosphere of the submarine.

Charon's soft cry wakened Father Ikanos from his slumbers in the soft armchair in his sacristy. He went out into the moonlit graveyard. The priest kissed the men on each cheek, much to Sandy's surprise, and shook their hands.

'Welcome, my friends, I have prayed for your safe arrival and the success of your mission. Come now, I will show you your hiding place for the day. I have put food, water and wine beside your bedding.'

The reverend father led the three men over to a new marble crypt. He slid open the grave-slab, which lay on greased, wooden rollers. He then lit and lowered a lantern to show them plates of olives, honey, bread, cheese and three bottles of dark red retsina wine. Sandy, Lofty and Charon carefully lowered the rucksacks containing the mines and detonators, then climbed into their hiding place. No sooner had their heads touched the rough bedding than each fell into a deep sleep.

Father Ikanos spent the day seemingly tending his grave-yard, weeding and pruning, but in reality was on the watch for the hated Germans and also carefully listening for any telltale snoring from his new flock.

Charon and his two companions slept, dosed and chatted throughout the day. Then, as darkness fell, they ate and drank heartily, before loading their baggage onto the donkey Father Ikanos had brought from the village.

The priest then led them through the dark night on footpaths over the hills in a gentle curve behind Heraklion until they reached the grove of tall canes which looked down over the hive of activity taking place on the airfield.

The next day they lay in the tarpaulin-covered hide Charon had chosen. They took it in turns to carefully watch and time the sentries' patrols while bomber after bomber arrived from German-occupied Greece. Each was waved into line in their squadrons where armourers waited with bomb-laden trolleys, ready to load them.

Late that night, while Charon watched ready to signal a warning, a black-faced Sandy crept between patrols and, with wire cutters, carefully snipped three sides of a rectangular panel in the fence. He then wired it back in place in such a way that it could not be spotted by the patrolling sentries.

Job done, he paced out a measured distance back from the fence, then came through the cane grove back out of sight of the guards. Sandy was careful to walk in a straight line directly from the control tower. The three of them had judged the distance from the fence to the tower within the airfield. Now they laid out six torches stuck upright into the sandy soil. The signal was the agreed distance signalled to Cairo and the lights would form a V, giving the bombers the direction to aim for.

Just after 1.30 am two RAF Lysander bombers from Egypt soared across the Oris Idi mountains and turned north-east. When they approached Heraklion, as anticipated, all the airfield lights were extinguished. Then the saboteurs switched on the signal torches, so giving the direction and distance for the planes to release their bombs.

Sandy, Lofty and Charon watched the chaos as loudspeakers boomed commands, the sentries fled to their shelters and all the airfield lights were turned off. As soon as this happened the three of them, with blackened faces, ran to the fence, pushed aside the snipped panel and each moved swiftly towards the four squadrons of Luftwaffe planes. Meanwhile the Lysanders had flown over their target, wheeled out over the sea, then turned to retrace their flight and began the attack.

Bombs exploded on and all around the control tower, offices and bomb shelters, as the saboteurs speedily fitted their limpet mines to plane after plane. They then darted back to escape through the fence.

As planned, the RAF planes wheeled again and came in firing their cannons into the blazing buildings, so keeping the Germans hiding under cover as Charon and his companions made their escape.

Erich Von Lichtoven led the first of the four squadrons. Two groups were JU 88s, the Stukas, well known for their terrifying, screaming attacks. The other two were HE 111 bombers, often described as the scourge of Europe.

It was 4.15 am. The raid had been meticulously planned, as was usual with Lichtoven. The plan was to meet up with the British convoy as it came within half an hour's sailing from Tobruk, and would therefore be seen by the surrounded Allied defenders. Erich thus hoped that the sight of the much-awaited relief convoy being totally destroyed would make the defenders lose heart and surrender to Rommel's forces.

Von Lichtoven was tired because of the hours of missed sleep due to the British bombers in the early morning, but now he felt exhilarated, ready to do his duty to his Führer. He could not believe their luck, due to the blithering incompetence of the attackers. Usually the RAF were to be respected, but to completely miss the dream target of his four flights, neatly lined up and armed by the runway, was incredible.

Attacking the control tower, offices and ammo dumps rather than the runways was just dumb. But maybe he himself could take some of the credit.

Erich had been woken out of a deep sleep by an only too familiar sound, the drone of heavy bombers approaching. His urgently yelled commands to turn off all airfield lights and not to use the searchlights, nor the anti-aircraft guns, were promptly acted on. So the airfield would have been in complete blackout if some fool had not left two desk lights on in the control tower, which became the centre of the attack.

'*Mein Gott*, that idiot will pay for his folly, but maybe not too badly,' he reconsidered, for the error may well have saved his planes.

As the rose-hued dawn glimmered to their left his mind ran over the plans for the attack, named 'Operation Cobra'. Admiral Canaris's intelligence staff had broken the codes the Royal Navy used to signal to their fleets in the Mediterranean. From this, together with information from one of their spies in Cairo, they learnt of the plans for a massive relief convoy to sail overnight from Malta to Tobruk to supply the beleaguered garrison.

The Germans knew the ships involved, which supplies were on board and the routes and timings planned. His four flights were to be met, one hour from the coast by an escort force of Messerschmitt Bf 109 fighters from the Africa Corps who would easily beat off any British attempts to disrupt his plans.

The attack would begin at 5.30 am precisely, led by the screaming Stukas who would disable the British ships and their escorts. Then Erich's heavy bombers would ensure the complete destruction of any survivors. The attack would then be seen by the bleary, defending sentries in Tobruk as they woke to another morning of blinding sunshine.

He looked back. The planes were in perfect order. Erich gave a quick radio check to each plane, they all responded in turn. Then he looked up and ahead for his escort.

'Ach, there they were, high above.'

The leading Messerschmitt waggled his wings as the dots

of the escorts formed a protective umbrella over Richter's bombers.

Heinrich Webb, a decorated fighter ace, scanned the skies ahead for the tiny gleam of reflected sunshine that would indicate an approaching RAF fighter plane. He saw nothing, and if these RAF boys had a go they were in for real trouble, his squadron was more than a match for them. Then he looked down in shock as the first bomber exploded.

One of the planes in the second flight just blew apart, and the explosion was so fierce that the two following bombers crashed into the debris and shattered out of the sky.

Then more planes began to explode. Startled, Von Lichtoven swivelled round and then barked into the radio, 'All planes, we must have been sabotaged, release your bombs now!'

The whole sky seemed to explode as, rather than save themselves, the pilots just triggered their own deaths.

Just with this event in mind the saboteurs had added belt and braces to their detonators. A thin wire attached between the lifting hook on the bomb's fin and the holding catch of the bomb release door also linked each. So that as the bomb fell, the detonator exploded.

Only two planes escaped the destruction due to faulty detonators but, seeing what had happened to their comrades, both pilots sensibly parachuted down to be captured by launches from the rescue convoy.

As the fighter pilots turned in despair back to their airfield in the desert it was almost as if they could hear the huge cheering from the British fleet and from General Montgomery's defenders in Tobruk.

When the news of this disaster reached Berlin and was nervously reported by Göring to Hitler, the Führer screamed invectives, glared at him then commanded, 'That is enough, this nest of vipers on Crete have had their last success. Our Gestapo chief there is obviously not German enough to bring these vicious peasants to heel. Replace him now with someone who will not allow another German life to be lost and who will strike terror into every Cretan heart!'

Chapter 21

Chania Seafront

May 1942

Crowds lined the entrance to Chania harbour. Marshalled by angry-faced Wehrmacht soldiers, they were pushed into a cordon around the bay where a line of young Cretan men and boys, hands tied behind their backs, waited for execution. Standartführer Schubert, the new head of the Gestapo, strutted to the front of his men.

'People of Chania. Last night your so-called resistance fighters helped the enemy to kill brave pilots from the Luftwaffe. You have been warned time and time again not to help these enemies of Germany, now you will see what happens and pay the price of your betrayal.'

Schubert stepped back into the crowd of high ranking officers. Lieutenant von Roon moved to take his place. Von Roon commanded the waiting firing squad to take aim. Just as he was about to say fire, a shot rang out and he collapsed to the ground. Chaos ensued. The young men seized their chance and either jumped into the bay or ran to hide in the crowd. The soldiers raised their rifles and scanned the nearby rooftops as the assassin's shot had come from on high.

Charon, dressed in full paratrooper's uniform, moved forward on the balcony on top of Hasan Pasha's ancient mosque. He yelled and signalled to the advancing soldiers,

'There he goes!' pointing up the main street leading away from the harbour.

He was dressed in the same uniform as the others guarding the rooftops. He was holding a Karabiner 98k rifle, the weapon of the paratroopers. Troops rushed away in the direction he had indicated. Charon came down the stone steps and joined the scurrying shambles of soldiery and civilians. He made his way along the seafront past the Nazi headquarters with its fluttering swastika and up the side of the barracks into Ritsou Street, then dived down the steps into the souvenir shop.

'Bloody Hell, Alexio! What a shock you gave me clattering in like that. Get yourself hidden quickly before they come searching.'

Andrea hauled the rug aside and opened the barrel door to the cellar next door. Charon climbed in, lay down on his palliasse and was soon sound asleep.

Chapter 22

Christmas Celebrations 1942

By now Charon was well known in Chania. Most of the people who worked in the bars, cafés and restaurants had met the young waiter from the Aphrodite Restaurant. Its owner, Uncle Demetrios of the great booming laugh, was of course extremely well known to all and very popular. They had heard the tragic tale about the young man's family and how the youth, they knew as Antoni, got his injuries. Often, as he limped away after a hard shift at work, he would be offered a seat to rest in and given a glass of his favourite drink, freshly pressed orange juice.

Antoni always seemed to have a smile and a joke for them. As well, he often had some fascinating snippets of gossip from overhearing German troops during his two jobs. The only things that puzzled them were why this young man was working in the headquarters of the hated Nazis, and how his limp and mental health seemed to improve in their company. Some assumed he was placed in his work by the resistance. Antoni just laughed when questioned and cleverly changed the subject.

Further along the seafront towards the jetty, just before the ancient Venetian, domed ship-building sheds, you find the *kafenion* Aetos (Eagle). This is where many of the fishermen come to have a coffee, a Metaxas brandy or a glass of ouzo, while exchanging news. The Germans were totally unaware it was also a gathering point for the Andartes when they visited their island's capital.

This popular meeting place, like many in Crete, had a clandestine radio. Here, in a back room with its sound turned low, men would gather and listen in to the broadcasts from the BBC. This was an offence punishable by execution but was the only way to get reliable news, rather than listen to the Germans' propaganda about the progress of the war.

The previous Christmas, Charon had listened with the others as all seemed to be going wrong. Barbarossa, the German blitzkrieg, had raced across vast distances in Russia, destroying all before them, and the Wehrmacht were at the very gates of Moscow. In North Africa, General Rommel had taken over from the inept Italian forces and was battering the Allies back through the deserts towards Egypt. Then on Sunday the 7th December 1941 the Japanese attacked Hawaii and shattered the American fleet at Pearl Harbour with a heavy, cowardly, unannounced attack. After that they took Singapore and seemed likely to become the masters of Asia. However, the Americans, with their massive military resources, were now very much in the war they had tried to avoid.

This Christmas things were totally different. The tide of war had turned in favour of the Allies. The Germans were losing the siege of Stalingrad where the epic Russian resistance was draining away their strength. In Egypt the new Allied commander, General Bernard Montgomery, had revitalised his forces and, after winning the battle of El Alamein, his tanks, artillery and planes were driving Rommel back west. Fortune at last seemed to have decided who the victors should be.

Britain's Prime Minister, Winston Churchill said:

Before Alamein, we never had a victory.
After Alamein, we never had a defeat.

So Charon, strongly supported by his Uncle Demetrios, felt it was time for him to take a short break and join his people as they celebrated Christmas.

Chania's main church, the Cathedral, stands in the centre of the town. If you walk just two blocks up the Halidon Street from the sea towards the bus station, turn into the square on your left. Stroll up the wide stone steps and make your way into the place of worship.

Inside, you soon begin to feel at peace in the tranquil atmosphere. Slim, yellow, tapered candles stand in a bed of sand in a brass tray, ready for you to light and make your blessing.

Father Corban pulled back the faded curtain to his private retreat. He turned, closed them and then sat down wearily on his chair to think through his plans for the coming weekend, one of the most important celebrations in the Coptic calendar. Even those of his flock who hardly ever came to church could be relied upon to turn up for Christmas. Deep in thought, his reverie was broken as a young Greek man limped into his sanctuary.

'*Kalispera*, Father, God be with you.'

'*Kalispera*, my son, but you should not be here, this room is sacred.'

'I know that well, Father, but I need your help, you will understand when I tell you, I am known as Charon.'

The old priest gasped. Could this young stripling, this simple-minded youth, who he knew worked as one of the waiters in the Aphrodite Restaurant owned by Demetrios, really be the assassin feared so much by the Germans who day and night were scouring the whole island, searching for him? His name was muttered by old men in their *kafenia*. Schoolchildren talked about him with awe. His exploits were the main topic of gossip in bars and the markets all over Crete.

'Tell me your story, my son, and I will see if I can be of help to you.'

Father Corban, who was now entering his seventy-eighth year, thought that by now he had heard all of the triumphs and tragedies of human experience as they take their various paths through life.

But never had he heard such a sad story from one so young. As Charon described his life so far the old priest looked deep into his eyes. What a grim determination emanated from this youth. What a terrible hatred drove him on his campaign of vengeance, for his family and for Crete.

As the tale drew to a close Father Corban placed his hand gently on Charon's shoulder and said, 'Before we talk further, my son, let us kneel in prayer for those you have lost and to seek God's forgiveness and support for all you have done and plan to do.'

Charon said that he knew how the old priest hated the Germans for the terror and brutality they had wreaked against his congregation. Also that he knew of the priest's links to the Andartes in the mountains and the British officers, with their radio operators and runners, who were increasingly waging a successful resistance campaign against the occupiers. He explained that, having heard of the marvellous change in the direction of the war in North Africa and Russia, he had decided just to take a short break away from his campaign of vengeance and celebrate Christmas with his own people.

'But, why here, Charon? Why not go back to your own village of Galatas and be with those of your family and friends who still live?'

'No, I cannot, Father, they would soon see through this disguise and recognise me. The Germans would inevitably find out, and my villager's lives and livelihoods would be put at risk. I have come to accept that I cannot return home until our war here is over.'

'Alright, my son, I understand. You are most welcome to join our service here tomorrow. But first please come to my home. Eat, drink and rest. Then you must come and join my congregation as we come together this weekend for the joyous celebration of the birth of our beloved saviour.'

Father Corban chanted out the familiar messages of hope to his crowded church. Then, just before midnight, all the lights were put out and they stood for a short time in quiet prayer. When the old bells in the tower started to clang the beginning of the new day, Father Corban lit a candle, held it aloft and shouted out, 'Hallejujah!'

As the people of Chania filed out, many of the mothers stopped to say 'Happy Christmas' and gave a hug and a kiss to the young man, Antoni, standing by their priest at the door.

Chapter 23

The Tunnel

July 1943

The road which connects the main towns on Crete's northern coast runs west to Kissamos. Here it turns south, right down to Elafonisi and Palaiochora. Halfway down, near the little village of Plagia, the road has been tunnelled through a shoulder of limestone rock which descends from the hills between the road and the sea.

Charon, ever conscious of the need not to concentrate his attacks just on and around Chania, decided to make this his next target. He loaded boxes of dynamite and landmines from his British friends into stout, strong straw panniers on Meagan his donkey. Then he led her up into the mountains. Travelling only at night, they made their way through valleys and over passes, due west. They skirted several small villages including Sebronas, Floria and Limni, then onwards until they reached the coastal road.

Charon guided Meagan up the hillside above the southern exit from the tunnel and offloaded his explosives, tools and equipment into a cleft in the rocks, well out of sight of any passer-by. After he had found a good hollow to make another temporary hide, Charon put his *panikryfto* in place, pegged it firmly with sharp twigs and placed some branches and small stones on top.

Over the next two days and evenings, Charon was hard at work. He waited until darkness fell, then took a rucksack full of explosive mines down the hillside and into the exit from the tunnel. He used a hammer and chisel to dig a staggered line of holes in the rocky floor of the tunnel. Into each he squeezed a landmine, then carefully replaced the grit around it, concealing them. A thin, strong cord was then fastened through the trigger-pins on the mines and fed back up into his hide. Next Charon went to the lip of the roof above the opening and buried several large bunches of dynamite there. Again a cord linked the detonators attached to each group and fed in under the *panikryfto*.

At the northern entrance to the tunnel there is a wide ledge above a steep ravine. The tunnel is single way, only wide enough for one vehicle or cart. People would wait here until they were sure the passageway was clear, before proceeding. Charon tied a stout rope around Meagan then lowered himself and a refilled rucksack down, until he was roughly his own height below the road.

He chiselled holes in the rock face and jammed his bombs into them. A third cord linking them was fed up the side and into bushes at the top where it was firmly tied to the trunk of a tree.

Now his trap was set. That same night he took Meagan down to Plagia's village square and tied her to the handle of the church door. A note attached to her saddle said:

Father, I have to leave my beloved island as the German beasts seek me. Please look after my donkey. She is hard-working and has been a good servant to me.

Charon

Charon had learnt in the Nazi headquarters that every Saturday morning an armoured car would lead two jeeps filled with soldiers from the barracks at Kissamos down the road to relieve the garrison keeping guard at Palioliora.

Early the next morning he woke, tied a second *panikryfto* to his back and, looping a rifle over his shoulder, made his way through the bushes and trees to the roof of the northern entrance to the tunnel. There he lay, waiting for the drone of engines.

The sky above was a perfect blue. Just a few gentle wisps of woolly cloud drifted. He inhaled the familiar scent of thyme and myrtle which melded with other mountain herbs as the overnight dew dried in the increasing heat of the sun. From all around him came a sweet chorus of song from little birds welcoming the new day.

Charon thought how strange life was, as he lay back drinking in the beautiful morning, while planning death and destruction to his enemies. His reverie was interrupted by the grumble of the armoured car and the whine of engines from the jeeps it escorted.

He made his way back through the bushes to where he had slept and took the two cords, one in each hand. As soon as he saw the bonnet of the armoured car appear in the exit, he heaved one cord which triggered the landmines and then pulled the other one, tied to the explosives on the roof, hard.

A mighty blast echoed out of the tunnel as the armoured car and the first jeep were thrown aloft then crashed down, destroyed, their occupants dead or severely injured. The second blast blew up the front of the hillside, which collapsed down, creating a huge cloud of dust and blocking the tunnel.

The jeep at the back reversed at full speed out of the tunnel and screeched onto the ledge. The sergeant in charge leapt out and radioed news of the disaster to Kissamos, who told him reinforcements would be sent as a matter of urgency. His men cautiously re-entered the tunnel to see if they could be of any help to their comrades.

Charon recrossed the tunnel's roof, crawled his way into the bushes above the entrance, and waited for more of his enemy to arrive. It took nearly one and a half hours before the column approached. A tank was in front of three lorries full of heavily armed Wehrmacht soldiers. They manoeuvred into the waiting area and filled the space beside the surviving jeep.

Oberst Paul Schneider jumped out to be briefed on what had happened as his soldiers lined up before him. Just as he turned to lead the men into the tunnel, Charon gripped and heaved on the cord which set off the dynamite in the cliff. The edge of the roadway collapsed. The tank, lorries and many of the troops hurtled down to their doom into the valley deep below.

None of the soldiers noticed Charon, who made his way through the shrubs, down the steep hillside and off towards his sanctuary in the mountains.

When the remaining troops carried out an inch by inch search of the hillside they found only the hiding place where he had left a cloth marked:

Chapter 24

Pigs

September 1943

Gefreite (corporals) Helmut Fischer and Wolfgang Bauer together with Sergeant Jurgen Metzger sat at the table outside the Aphrodite Restaurant. They quaffed stein after stein of pale yellow lager imported from Hamburg.

The soldiers believed this was a well-earned break after their recent long campaign up in the mountains. For nearly five weeks they had chased gangs of Andartes up gorges, through ravines and climbed after them up the rugged Cretan mountains. Only occasionally did they even catch a glimpse of these bandits who knew the rugged terrain like the back of their hands. This was mainly when a small group of them would wait behind in ambush, covering the other's retreat.

After a while, failure and frustration caused them to unleash their anger on more than twenty of the small mountain villages who were without doubt supporting the resistance and passing information to their fighters. In village after village the same terror descended. Men, women and children, no matter of what age or how they protested their innocence, were herded together, often into their local church.

Then a proclamation against them signed by the German Kommandant, Major General Heinrich Muller, was read out. After that, they were either shot or burnt alive in their place of

111

worship. This massacre became known as 'The Holocaust of Viannoss'.

Over 500 local people lost their lives. Their villages were destroyed together with their animals and crops. Muller believed that this would discourage others from resistance. He was wrong. All this achieved was to inflame further hostility.

The smell from the burning corpses of the villagers they had slaughtered would be with these three soldiers for a long time, no matter how much they drank to forget.

Now they decided to match their beer with glasses of schnapps. Fischer called out their order to the young, lame waiter they called Antoni. As he brought forth the foaming glasses and a bottle of the German spirit, Charon's expression froze as he heard what they were saying about the lovely, young Cretan beauty walking along the jetty in front of them. She ignored their wolf whistles as, blushing, Melina increased her speed.

Charon's face darkened as he overheard them describing in graphic detail what they would like to do to the young woman. He placed their drinks in front of them with the bill, and then went back to the waiter's station. Charon reached under the cutlery table for the fully loaded revolver always kept there, when his Uncle Dimitrios said, 'Don't be a fool, Alexio, not here, not now. You will find a way of wreaking vengeance on these swine.'

At lunchtime the next day the same three Germans came back and sat at their usual table. After serving them drinks Charon said in broken, clumsy German, 'Gentlemen, yesterday I could not help but notice your interest in the young Cretan girl who walked past you. Would you like to meet her?'

'Bloody right, we would!' said Corporals Fischer and Bauer. Sergeant Metzger excused himself as he was shortly to go on sentry duty.

Charon led the other two along the quayside past the line of crowded restaurants and tavernas, by the main barracks, and into Ritsou Street. He stopped at the souvenir shop and said, 'Gentlemen, she works here, in her father's shop. Her name is Melina, and she will be very pleased to meet you. Melina is always very ready to give a warm welcome and be rewarded by German soldiers.'

Their eyes gleamed as they went down the stone stairs and into the souvenir shop. Melina and Andrea were waiting behind the counter as planned.

'Welcome, welcome, German soldiers,' said Andrea. 'Come, sit, make yourselves comfortable while my daughter goes next door to prepare to greet you in her own way.

'Have a glass of raki while you wait. I make it myself in my village up in the mountains. Although I say so myself, everyone tells me it is excellent, the finest in all Crete.'

Three large glasses of strong raki later, combined with the very powerful sleeping draught Andrea had added, took effect. A very unsteady Corporal Bauer pulled aside the curtain and staggered into the bedroom next door. Melina stood there, slim and very beautiful. Her long, raven-black hair cascaded down her slim back. She wore a dark blue, low-cut silk dress. Melina smiled at the soldier who moved forward to embrace her. Then Charon, who had sneaked into the bedchamber through its window, struck him hard with a club made out of olive wood. Bauer collapsed unconscious and was heaved into concealment alongside the bed.

After about a quarter of an hour Melina stepped back into the shop and beckoned to the other soldier. Corporal Fischer was now very much the worse for wear. He could hardly stand so the girl and her father helped him in to where he met the same fate as his comrade.

That night Charon and Andrea, now in dressed in Wehrmacht uniforms, drove the Nazi jeep they had stolen to the local slaughterhouse. Andrea had arranged with his friends that the gate would be left unlocked. They drove in, and then they used the animal hoist to remove the deeply unconscious soldiers and place them on marble butchering tables. There each soldier's throat was cut and the fountain of blood allowed to drain away. The corpses were hoisted back into the rear of the jeep, together with a huge, hairless, pink sow that had been hanging on a hook waiting its turn with the knife.

The jeep, now a hearse, then twisted and turned through the tiny alleyways behind the main seafront. Then it drove into a narrow lane which led to the front of the German barracks. Here Charon and Andrea stopped to arrange the message to their hated foe.

The two soldiers, still dressed in full uniform, were placed upright on the driver's and the passenger's seats. A flag was wrapped around the naked pig, which was put between them with each soldier's arms tied tightly around it, in a weird mortal embrace.

On guard by the closed gate to the barracks were three sentries, one of whom was Sergeant Jurgen Metzger. He screamed out a warning as one of their jeeps hurtled out of the darkness straight towards them. Charon had jammed a large rock on the accelerator pedal, tied the steering wheel in place and then released the brake.

The jeep crashed through the wooden gate, careened across the parade ground and smashed into a low stone wall, its engine still roaring. The sentries ran swiftly to it and switched off the ignition. Metzger's face turned an unhealthy pallor of yellow-white as he recognised his two drinking mates and the horrific tableau of their death.

Lieutenant Von Klein dashed to the front of the wreck to see what the soldiers were gazing at so intently. Two of his soldiers, very dead, each hugged a huge naked pig which was wrapped in a Nazi flag and lolled on the dashboard. A message tied to the front of the jeep said:

These swine insulted the women of Crete.
This is the fate that awaits any of you who do the same.
Get off our island.
Go home, back to your pigsties.

Central Crete

Chapter 25

Kidnap

Charon opened the glass door to the little shrine where the villagers lit candles to Saint Gerasimos. Neatly folded under the statue of the Saint was a message from O' Tom. It read:

> I have important news for you and need your help. Can you please meet me at the place we first met, at 11 pm on Thursday next week?

Charon knew that this meant two days and three hours later than stated in case the message fell into enemy hands. So at 2 am on Saturday he sat, waiting in the Old Mill.

Tom Dunbabin explained that the Allied commander in Cairo had been very impressed at the way the resistance campaign, including Charon's work, was striking fear into German hearts. They also had given approval to an audacious plan cooked up by him and Paddy Leigh Fermor, another of the key officers in the British Secret Services. The scheme was to kidnap the commander of the German forces in the Heraklion region and take him by submarine as a captive to Cairo. They had hoped it would be Major General Heinrich Muller whose cruelty had made him so hated on the island, but he had now been replaced by Major General Heinrich Kreipe, who would be taken instead.

'How can I be of help, O' Tom?'

'We intend to set up an ambush on the road between his headquarters near Heraklion and Villa Adriane, by Knossos, where he sleeps. Then, that night to take him into the mountains and onwards to reach the south coast near Rodakino. The Germans will be furious and send out many soldiers seeking us which, together with their spotter planes, will make our escape very difficult. We will of course use caves to shelter us during the day and travel only at night.

'You know our route like the back of your hand from your hunting days. Could you please act as our secret escort, staying a good distance away, and doing whatever you can to confuse and disrupt our pursuers?'

'It would be an honour, O' Tom.'

The idea for the kidnapping had been inspired by an event some time back. The first overall commander of 'The Fortress of Crete' was General Andrea. He ordered a well-known Cretan hunter, Manoussos Manoussakis, to take him to shoot ibex in the Lefka Ori mountains. Manoussos, seeing the opportunity for a great coup, contacted the resistance and suggested kidnapping him. Special Operations Executive (SOE) in Cairo approved the plan, but for various reasons it could not be carried out.

So on the 4th February 1944, a plane set out from Alexandria carrying Major Patrick Leigh Fermor (PLF) and a team of saboteurs. PLF parachuted down to the agreed dropping zone in the Lasithi mountains successfully. He was then to signal the others to follow, but a thick mist descended and the drop had to be abandoned. After several more attempts which also had to be called off it was decided to send the others by sea. Also the Germans had become suspicious about the increased radio traffic and the number of over-flights at night, so they reinforced their garrisons in the south.

Weeks passed before a launch containing PLF's comrade, Captain Billy Moss, and two famous resistance leaders, Manoli Paterakis and George Tyrakis, landed safely on Crete's southern coast near Tsoutsouros.

After a feast of barbecued goat the group set off for their hideout in the mountains. Here they were joined by Kapitän Athanaslos Bourdzalis, an elderly resistance fighter but of great strength and reputation. Athanaslos had also got to know the German General's driver and guard so knew the locations very well. PLF himself spent a few days reconnoitring the site of the ambush, by a sharp curve in the road. The group then moved into position in hiding by the road. It was five days before the best opportunity presented itself. At 9 pm on the 26th April, PLF and Captain Moss stood, in German uniforms, and signalled to the General's driver to stop. They then said they needed to inspect papers. When the driver protested, two Andartes ran out from cover and heaved him out of the car. Meanwhile PLF had General Kreipe covered with his Colt revolver. Then he too was unceremoniously evicted and handcuffed.

The General was bundled into the rear of the car where three Andartes menaced him with their wickedly sharp Cretan hunting knives as they sat on top of him. The car by now was driven by Moss while PLF sat in the passenger seat wearing the General's hat and jacket. They made their way to Villa Adriane where the sentries clicked smartly to attention, saluted, then gazed in amazement as the General sped past. Shortly after, they were slowed to a walking pace in Heraklion as soldiers came out from a cinema, but PLF just returned their salutes and without any trouble the car left, on the road to Rethymnon. About halfway along the twisty road they got out just after Drosia village. Moss, the General and the Andartes headed off in the direction of Anoyeia to their hideout on the slopes of Mount Ida.

PLF and one of the fighters took the car to the coast near the village of Panorma. Here they dumped it but deliberately left Royal Navy cigarette tins and items of equipment to conceal the support from the resistance and make the Germans think they had escaped by sea. They then pinned a message onto the front seat of the General's car where it could not be missed, which read:

This operation was conducted by a British Commando supported by soldiers of the Royal Greek Army in the Middle East. So any reprisals against civilians would be pointless, unjust and in breach of International Law. We are sorry we cannot take your motor car. We shall meet again soon.

Major Leigh Fermor

The German headquarters in Chania was a hive of activity. A full alert had been called. Standartführer Schubert, the head of the Gestapo, had taken charge of the mission to find and save their General. He drew three thick lines which covered the main valleys through the mountains leading to the southern coast. Their forces were marshalled on each route with the plan being that, as they advanced, patrols would peel off and climb the adjacent mountains where the kidnappers would inevitably hide.

Charon served coffee to them as he listened intently to their plans. He knew that they did not have enough men to completely cover the vast terrain. Their hope was that, as soon as any soldiers found evidence or saw the captors, all forces could concentrate on that route.

The actual escape plan was to take to the mountains just above the Germans' most westerly search area. Charon decided it would be best therefore to try to mislead them into thinking the escapers had taken the left hand route across the island, that is, the one furthest east.

That night Charon sped south, dressed in German uniform on a stolen motorbike.

Over the next three days radio messages back to Chania reported Charon's false trail. Under intensive questioning a villager in Kerasia had said he had seen some men high up on the mountains. The next night a sentry guarding the site by Prinias, where his patrol had camped overnight, was found with a cut throat. Then, when the soldiers tried to start their lorries and jeeps, they found that the fuel had been contaminated by sand. Now efforts concentrated on the area around Agios Ioannis.

One of the Fieseler Storch reconnaissance planes noticed a gleam from something at the edge of a mountain pass. He radioed in the information then wheeled round to fly slower and lower over it. As he approached what turned out to be a glinting, highly polished belt buckle, Charon, well hidden under his *panikryfto*, carefully sighted the sniper rifle then shot the pilot through the windscreen.

The patrol sent to investigate the wreckage climbed a steep ravine towards where the plane had crashed. Just before they reached the edge, the dynamite Charon had buried exploded, sending a deadly avalanche of shattered rock down upon them.

By now Schubert the Gestapo chief was apoplectic. He commanded that all forces must now move to cover the eastern escape route, thus leaving the way virtually clear for Leigh Fermor's group and their captive General.

Charon's work was done. That night he jogged up and down the mountain slopes to the west until he reached the cliffs above Rodakino Bay. He was just in time. The submarine was starting to head out towards Egypt. But Captain Moss and Major Patrick Leigh Fermor stood in the conning tower and waved their grateful thanks to their own ferryman.

Over the next month O' Tom and his Andartes worked hard spreading the rumour that General Kreipe had planned the whole event so that he could escape to the Allies rather than the possibility of facing another winter in Russia.

Chapter 26

Sharks in the Mediterranean

May 1944

The Kubbelwagon rolled to a halt by the groves of bamboo fronting Aptera beach. The platoon stopped singing, leapt one by one over the tailboard and jogged down the dusty path.

All of them had been looking forward to this break for ages. They had talked about their favourite spot as they wearily climbed up and down the rugged terrain. They had searched for weeks chasing the elusive bandits up the Lefka Ori, the White Mountains, hunted them across the Askifou plateau and over the mountains above Rethymnon, but each time they got near enough to sniff them the Andartes would disappear like will-o'-the-wisps.

At least they had found one of the hideouts, a cave with a still smouldering fire and marks where it appeared one of the precious radio sets had been sited. But their prey had fled. If a radio set had been there it would have been operated by one of the accursed British SOE from Cairo. To capture one of these invaluable targets and hand him over to the Gestapo would have earned them more than a break by the sea, maybe even some leave back home. Though, with the tales of increasing bombing raids by the RAF and the Americans, even that might not have been worth it.

Stripping off their dusty uniforms they ran, naked, yelling

with delight into the warm, azure Mediterranean. After fooling around a bit, Axel, their sergeant, led the swimmers out to sea, his powerful crawl easily outpacing them. Axel turned onto his back at the mouth of the bay and looked back to see how his comrades were progressing. They were a good bunch and had been through a lot together. He looked up into the blue sky and remembered back to the fear of parachuting down through unbelievably intensive flak into the fiercest firefight he had ever experienced, and would ever wish to be involved in.

Hans and Karl were catching up, coming towards him now, but of course fat Meindl was trailing in the rear. He really must get him on the exercise ground again and get some of that sausage and beer weight off him. God knows when they would have to fight again or where, the way the war was going.

'What's that?' he yelled.

A black fin was closing in on Meindl.

Ach, just one of the men fooling to scare him. Of course there were no sharks in the Mediterranean Sea. Wait a minute, all the rest were by now treading water around him, also looking back. There was no one missing!

Just then Meindl let out a terrible scream and, threshing his fat arms, sank below the sea. The soldiers watched in awe as he burst forth onto the surface again. There was a huge gash across his chest and stomach. Blood fountained up with the spume as Meindl disappeared again under the sea and did not come up again.

Axel was about to swim back when the black fin reappeared, this time heading steadily and purposefully towards them.

'Get out of here!' he screamed and plunged out to sea, round the point, to the next cove.

Two of the soldiers managed to scramble up the steep head-land from where they yelled, 'Faster!' as the fin appeared to be gaining on their mates. Then the swimmers reached the land and staggered up onto the wet sand. In their terror they did not notice the shards of broken glass scattered across the tideline.

From the rocks Karl and Hans watched, horrified, as their entire platoon clutched their feet, which were now streaming with blood then, in disbelief, as the deadly toxin had its effect and the soldiers screamed, vomited and collapsed over in rigours of agonising death. The two survivors ran as fast as they could to their lorry and away to get help.

Two hours later the beach was surrounded with a grim, closely packed cordon of heavily armed Wehrmacht who started moving slowly through the groves of tall bamboo towards the sea. A fast patrol boat creamed up and down the bay, machine guns swinging, ready to blast at any movement.

Kapitän von Hoffman waved the men forward from the turret of his armoured car then signalled his driver to move on down the track, guns swaying from side to side seeking a target.

Charon stood, hidden by the tall fronds, just where the access track emerged onto the sand. He had dumped the fin and the vicious razor-sharp sickle in the sea. His flippers lay behind a rock concealed from the boats.

He waited just until the armoured car moved ahead of the line of troops then squeezed the trigger of the Panzerfaust anti-tank rocket. The armoured car exploded, shooting Kapitän von Hoffman up into the air.

Startled, the soldiers moving forward did not notice the thin tripwire and staggered across it. Charon had placed bunches of plastic explosive, grenades and cans of petrol in a ring across the canes. Crashing booms reverberated as bursts of flame ignited the bone-dry cane grove into a blazing, deathly inferno. Very few survived the cataclysm, and most of these were so badly burnt that they died on the way to, or in, hospital.

Charon slipped silently back into the sea, concealed by the dense pall of noxious smoke. Underwater he swam round the point to where a cliff fell vertically into the sea. Diving deeper he entered the underwater cave he had discovered with his brother long ago. The boys had been searching for octopus when, behind a seaweed-curtained rock they found the hidden entrance. Charon rose onto a dry ledge of rock, stripped off the frogman's suit, towelled himself down roughly and climbed up into the hammock strung above the rocks. Straight away he fell into a deep, exhausted sleep. Outside the noise of catastrophe died away and the sea lapped gently once again.

The next day orders were issued to all the German forces cancelling all relaxation on the beaches. One more pleasant avenue of escape was closed to the increasingly fearful and hated occupiers of Crete.

Chapter 27

The Butcher

August 1944

Standartenführer Schubert knew well how soldiers who saw, the by now famous, Melina were almost instantly smitten. Curious to see this renowned beauty, he took to occasionally popping in to her father Andrea's shop. He was amassing quite a number of Cretan souvenirs until one evening she came in from the back room to serve him in Andrea's absence. She knew well who he was and of his reputation as "The Butcher of Crete". Trying to conceal her dislike, she served him politely then cleverly deflected his attempt to chat to her by saying, 'Oh, excuse me, Sir, it is time to phone my Uncle, who is at the taverna.'

Schubert walked slowly back to his quarters in a fever of lust. He just had to have that beautiful maiden, but how? He failed to notice the young man who had been following him.

By this time it was Charon's third winter working as a waiter between the Aphrodite Restaurant and the Gestapo headquarters in Chania. So he was well known to all the Germans. They took little notice of this lame simpleton who at least seemed efficient enough in bringing in their orders for food, drink and fresh coffee.

In three days' time Charon got the order he had been waiting for. One large cream coffee and two pastries to be delivered directly to Schubert's private office. The German Gestapo chief did not even raise his head from his paperwork, just grunted.

He was completely taken aback when the young man they all knew as Antoni said in a trembling voice in broken German, 'Pardon me, Sir, may I speak to you?'

'What is it?'

'My cousin Melina works in her father Andrea's shop in Ritsou Street. I understand you have been there and met her. She told me that she had sensed that you had liked her looks and may even wish to get to know her better, and no wonder, she is such a beauty that men all ove—'

'Well, so what? Get on with it!' Schubert barked.

'Oh, you see, Melina knows that you are an extremely important officer in the German army and have great powers.'

Schubert pretended not to enjoy this flattery.

'Melina's boyfriend and now fiancée is a prisoner in your cells charged with terrorist offences of which he is of course innocent. She is extremely frightened that he may be executed for crimes he did not commit. Melina would be prepared to do anything to have him released.'

'Anything?'

'Yes, Herr Hauptmann, anything.'

Schubert asked for the man's name, said he would look into the case and that the waiter should return in three days at 11 am.

Charon arrived promptly and, after further questioning, Schubert said that the boyfriend would be released at 8 am the following morning. The waiter should be by the back door to take him away, and that Melina should come to Schubert's bedroom at 10.30 pm that night. He would notify the guards to expect her. It was so agreed.

At the appointed hour that evening, Melina, wearing a cloak

to hide her head, nervously approached the two sentries standing at attention by the stout wooden doors of Gestapo headquarters. One of them winked at his companion then guided Melina in and explained she should take three flights of stairs to the topmost floor where Schubert had his suite of private apartments. The other sentry phoned up to Schubert to say she had arrived and was on her way.

The Gestapo chief splashed another dose of the powerful but sickening pomade onto his fleshy jowls and loosed the belt of his scarlet silk dressing gown, all that he wore.

Melina gained the top floor and walked towards the door to the suite. Schubert, who had been suspicious and cautious all of his life, watched carefully as she crossed the floor, through a little see-through cut in the door of his apartment. He did not see Charon, who, having killed the sentry posted on the roof, had come down through the hatch above the stairs and was standing pressed tightly into the wall on the right hand side of the door.

In response to her timid knock Schubert swept the door aside saying, 'Welcome, my dear.' His smile changed to fear when a slim, black-clad and masked figure pushed Melina aside and thrust a gun into his neck.

'One word, one cry of warning, and I shoot. Do you understand?'

Schubert nodded as he was pressed back onto the downturned bed. The young man then tied his ankles and wrists to each of the four bedposts.

'Do you know who I am?'

Schubert's face showed realisation combined with terror.

'Not Charon?'

'Yes, Butcher of my Cretans, we meet face to face at last.'

Charon told of the Germans' savagery that had cost him his

family; of the hatred he felt at the atrocities committed after the invasion and in villages all over Crete since; and of how he had nothing to lose in his campaign of vengeance but his worthless life.

Schubert looked into the cold, merciless eyes and began to plead not to be killed. He gave Charon details of planned raids on resistance groups, also plans to detect the British radio operators. He listed the names of the few of his informers who had still not been discovered, and said he would promise anything if Charon would let him live.

'No, the crimes you have committed against my people deserve at least ten executions. I pronounce you guilty and sentence you to death.'

As Schubert opened his mouth to scream for help, Charon jammed a rag in it, wrapped a pillow around his pistol and shot him once in the centre of his forehead. The pillow successfully masked the sound of the bullet, which ended the Butcher's life.

Charon made his way down two flights of stairs while strapping grenades from his satchel underneath the steps. He took a long, strong cord and carefully fastened it to each of the eyes on the pins of the grenades, then secured it as a trip-wire where the stairway was particularly gloomy. He made his way back into the bedroom. Charon untied the restraints from Schubert and attached a notice firmly to his chest with a Cretan dagger.

Then, removing a long coil of rope from around his waist, Charon tied it under the corpse's armpits. He tugged and heaved the body as it slithered across the floor to the large wide-open window. Just below the windowsill a flagpole jutted out from the wall bearing a huge swastika, the most hated emblem in Crete.

Charon firmly tied the end of the rope round the wooden pole, then slowly lowered the dead body so that it dangled below the flag of oppression. He then mounted the last short flight of stairs to the roof where Melina was waiting for him. He said, 'It is done.'

The pair then crept out onto the roof, past the dead sentry and made their way over the adjacent properties' roofs until they entered the hatch in the top of the building whose ground floor was Andrea's shop.

Meanwhile below, the two sentries were fantasising and discussing what was going on in their chief's boudoir. They wondered who the young lady was. Both had just caught a glimpse of flashing beauty under the hood. One cursed as something splattered onto his helmet.

'Bloody birds,' he cursed, looking upwards. Then, with horror, he saw the figure hanging from the flagpole dripping blood. 'Sound the alarm!' he yelled.

The guardroom emptied as well-armed soldiers ran after their officer up the stairs. He did not notice the tripwire and died in a tremendous, repeated explosion, which brought down two flights of stairs, then the third collapsed, bringing parts of the wall away. Only two soldiers survived, but they were badly wounded.

The fire engine's ladder proved too short to reach the corpse. So engineers started building a scaffold up the outside of the building. At last it reached high enough to grab, then cut through, the dangling rope.

They tied another, longer, one to it and lowered the body to the ground. By this time dawn had arrived, as had a growing crowd of curious fishermen. The soldiers and the locals easily read the notice stabbed into the hated Gestapo chief's chest. It said:

Beware, Germans,
As thus ends the life
Of 'The Butcher of Crete'.
So your lives will end
Unless you leave
Our beloved island.

Charon

At about the same time, the alerted sentries at the north-western exit road from Chania heard the rumble of cart wheels.

'Ach, it's only old Uncle Andrea going to the tip again.'

Charon and Melina lay, silent and still, under the false bottom of the cart. Even though it had been well constructed, the stench from the garbage pervaded their space so they pressed their mouths tightly to the holes cut in the floor, to breathe in the clean, fresh air of the morning. Later, much later in their lives, they would both join in laughter as they remembered where they had first pledged their love to one another.

Chapter 28

Jailbreak

September 1944

Charon sat by the waiter's station in the Aphrodite Restaurant. He mused on how things had changed since he started his campaign. Also how the beginning was so fresh in his mind that it could have been yesterday. But no, it was three years now since Charon made his presence known with the assassination of the Kommandant. If he stood up, he could look along the crowded quayside and see the very spot where his arrow had not only ended a life but also started the terror which was one of the main subjects of conversation he would overhear in this restaurant or in the Nazi headquarters. The soldiers were, as he had planned, increasingly scared of going out on patrol or taking their turn on sentry duty, particularly in the velvet dark of the Cretan night.

Now, however, the talk was also about the dramatic change in Germany's war. In Stalingrad, North Africa, the war at sea for the Atlantic and now, increasingly, the war in the Far East. The Allied forces were piling success onto success. Italy had surrendered and Allied forces were fighting their way up through that long peninsula, heading towards Germany and another type of final solution. It was obvious, even to the most ignorant Wehrmacht soldier, that the war would be lost. It was just a matter of time.

Now on Crete they were very thinly stretched, having had to take over the eastern end of the island when the Italian allies packed it in. They were constantly under pressure to release soldiers and equipment for battlefields elsewhere. Needless to point out it was always the best of their declining strength which was called for. Everyone dreaded the prospect of being posted to the icy wastes of the Russian steppes. The fighting in Italy was also very fierce and there, as in first Crete, Greece, then Russia, their armies were having to fight off the local resistance fighters as well as regular forces.

Charon listened and absorbed all this useful information to be passed on later to the Kapitäns and the Allied special forces. His arrangements for communication were much improved. There were now four locations in and around Chania where he or the resistance would leave coded messages arranging meetings. Now it was time again. The previous week, one of the Andartes had collected a note for Tom Dunbabin which had been left under a drainage cover near the mosque. That evening Charon and O' Tom met in the cellar of the Aetos, Uncles Andrea and Dimitrios's favourite tavern.

The Gestapo now knew well it was regularly used by some of the best known rogues in Chania and suspected it was one of the places where secrets were exchanged. They had made irregular sudden searches but somehow they always seemed to be expected and a more peaceful scene of old men drinking, playing cards and chatting would be difficult to envisage. The clandestine radio was very well hidden, as was the entrance to the old cellar.

The British officer and the Greek youth were by now great friends and respected one another hugely. So after a very enjoy-able discussion on the way things were proceeding, O' Tom said, 'Right, my young friend. You called for this meeting and said it was urgent. How can I help?'

'Thank you, O' Tom. I have learnt that many of the Gestapo swine are to be evacuated back to Germany shortly. They have decided that there will be one final act of vengeance to display their hatred of my people.

'Next week there will be an announcement calling the citizens of Chania to gather in front of the main barracks at the end of the harbour to hear an extremely important announcement.

'They plan to gather the resistance fighters they hold as prisoners and, one by one, lead them to the ramparts where their detested flag flies over our town. Each one of our brave Andartes will then be hurled, tightly bound, into the sea. As if this is not terrible enough they have amongst those they captured Perikles Vandoulakis, who you know well to be one of our greatest Kapitäns. He has managed with my help to conceal his real identity so far.'

'My God, you would think even these animals would by now be scared of their own skins as we will make sure they are punished in the courts for the bestiality they have carried out. What can we do?'

'I plan to assist them in breaking out of jail early in the morning of their planned execution.'

'What, all of them?'

'Yes, every single one of the twenty-three Andartes they hold, but I need your assistance. Here is what I plan. All the resistance fighters are kept segregated from the other prisoners. They have a single wing in the jail below the guards' living quarters. There are some forty cells in two rows with a central corridor. When visitors call they are taken down the stairs from where the soldiers sleep, to a landing where they are questioned by two sentries.

'Inside are the offices, a room which is used for interrogation, that is, a torture chamber, then the main guardroom which looks out onto the corridor and the cells.

'Throughout the night, there are only six men on duty. Two on the landing, two normally taking turns with the others to snooze, one always watching the cells and his comrade who every so often walks down the corridor, checking all is well. They are on a six-hour shift from midnight before they are relieved at 6 am.

'They know me as Antoni, the waiter from the Aphrodite. I take jugs of hot coffee to them at the start and end of their shift.

'They are of course bored out of their minds, the normal conditions for those on guard duty. They do not have a difficult time with their captives, a lot of their bravery and strength has been beaten out of them. My plan is that their coffee will be laced with a very strong sleeping draught that I know you can supply to me.

'I will stay chatting to them as I often do. They are always very ready to talk and hear gossip, particularly anything to do with women. By this means I will be sure that if any of them becomes alarmed as the drug begins to take effect on him or his comrades, I will deal with him.

'Then, at roughly 3 am, two of your men dressed as Gestapo officers and fluent in German will come to the entrance and ask to be let in. They will explain that, following a fresh lead, they need to urgently interrogate one of the prisoners. I will have telephoned to the soldiers at the entrance to advise them to expect these visitors. After they are safely in I will disable the phones and radios in the prison.

'We will release the prisoners, demanding that they keep total silence until our charade is over. The guards will be securely tied and gagged, then handcuffed to the bars of one of the cells. They can have one each, we would not wish them to be uncomfortable, eh?'

'My heavens, Charon, you have really thought this through. What an incredible advantage to have you, fluent in German, right in the very nerve centre of the beasts' lair. OK, so what next?'

After Charon had described in thorough detail how the escape would take place, Tom Dunbabin roared with glee and nearly crushed Charon in a bear hug.

'Charon, this is brilliant. We cannot, no, we will not fail. What a great plan. How it will damage what's left of the Nazi swines' morale, and what a fantastic end to your work as the ferryman of the dead!'

It all proceeded as planned. At 3 am the guards at the main entrance let the two 'Gestapo' officers in and directed them to the stairs which led to the prison. Roughly an hour later a line of tired, but joyful, Andartes were led through a small service door to an alley in the rear of the building. Then they all climbed up and squeezed into the back of a waiting lorry. Quietly it made its way round to the quayside to where the German patrol boats were berthed.

Half an hour before they arrived, the other half of Charon's plan had taken place. Ever since the Germans took over control of Chania, the early morning Cretan fishing fleet had been escorted out to sea by two powerful, well-armed German patrol boats. The arrangement was that at 5 am the fishing boats would make their way out of the harbour mouth to a position about 1/2 mile from the lighthouse. Here they would rendezvous with their escorts. Today was exactly the same as any other, or so the fishermen assumed.

Unbeknown to them, about half an hour prior to departure, two small rowing boats, full of Andartes who were armed to the teeth, rowed quietly up to the stern of each of the German launches. They were resistance fighters but also, in more peaceful times, very experienced seamen. One of them shimmied up the anchor thwart and disabled the snoozing sentry. Then the others embarked and, without any to do, disarmed and tied up the German crew. The Germans were then dragged up the gangway and into the waiting lorry. The hapless, tightly bound and gagged crews were then taken into the boathouses and secured to mooring rings.

Now all was set. The released resistance fighters climbed aboard and moved below decks to lie down and rest.

At the normal time Charon, posing as the officer in charge of the leading patrol craft, radioed to the German control room and then to the guard post on top of the lighthouse. Using the correct codes and the names of those on duty, he checked in and stated they were off to sea as usual.

The launches chugged out of the harbour, rendezvoused with the Chania fishing fleet beside the islet with the little white church which used to be a leper colony, and set off out into the Mediterranean.

But not all was the same. The captains of the fishing boats saw a small boat with a powerful motor leaving their escort which then sped round all of them bearing this message:

Gentlemen, we have been required by our HQ in Chania to carry out a search to the west where we are informed a group of terrorists may be planning more evil and destruction. Please proceed to fish as normal then return to the harbour.

Heil Hitler

The two launches sped off at top speed to the west. They motored on to the island called Agii Theodori. This place had been occupied in the far past, back to Minoan times, but now was only used by shepherds along the coast to provide a safe home and shelter for their goats. These sturdy creatures can easily survive without the humans who come over twice a year for milk, cheese and the young kids. However, there are still the stone ruins of an old village on the northern side, facing away from the mainland. These had been tidied, cleaned and equipped with fresh bedding, food and drink. One of the doctors trusted by the resistance and a nurse waited there to help the wounded.

All of them stayed there for ten days before the hue and cry died down and they could be taken at night by boat back to the mainland and on to their homes.

After the Andartes were safely ashore, Charon and Kapitän Perikles piloted the two German launches to a position above a deep trench known to the local fisherman and opened the scuttle cocks. The boats sank slowly into the depths as the two men rowed their way back to the mainland shore near to Platanias.

They made their way up to the Kapitän's village in the mountains. After a tremendous welcome they hugely enjoyed the villagers' hospitality, feasted mightily, then collapsed into the deep sleep of the victorious. Now Antoni and Charon were no more, they had served their purposes well.

Chapter 29

Victory

October 1944

The Aetos taverna was bursting at the seams. It seemed that the whole of Chania was one huge, exuberant, brilliant party. Thousands of the capital's inhabitants, together with many more from outside the town, had come to celebrate their victory and liberation.

In agreement with the Allies the German troops remaining on the island had retreated from Heraklion and Rethymnon and were gathered together in their barracks and camps in Chania. The mood against them could easily have turned ugly as people thought of taking vengeance on their vicious occupiers. But they were not allowed near them so thankfully everyone joined the biggest party the town had ever known instead.

In the taverna a group gathered to listen as one of their favourite poets chanted out familiar *mantinades*.

In the still of the night Charon will come.
Lie scared and shivering, German soldiers,
Terrified, trembling and sweating on your beds;
In the dark night Charon will come for you.

The Eagle of our beloved Kriti
Has extremely sharp talons.

Nazi scum, invaders of our island,
Now your time has come;
Charon hunts in the night.

As cheers broke out a group of the leaders left their raucous friends at the bar and went into a quieter area at the rear where they began discussing what was to happen next. Apart from getting their Boche prisoners off the island, there were also problems getting food and water distributed effectively to suffering villagers in the hinterland. Then talk turned to politics.

It was already clear, from events on the Greek mainland, that the various communist groups were now uniting in a common effort to take over power.

At the table were seated the most important Kapitäns and also the senior Allied officers, including Tom Dunbabin and Patrick Leigh Fermor from the Secret Services, who had been a huge help to the resistance. The officers vowed Allied support to the Kapitäns of the Andartes in the time ahead. They were just getting down to serious, detailed planning, when there was a commotion at the door which opened to the harbour.

A tall, slim, dark-haired Greek youth had tried to enter but was accosted by a group of Andartes who were, by now, full of both kinds of spirit.

'Hey you, where do you think you are going? Here's another one, lads! Another of the many men who now come out from wherever they have been hiding over the years of struggle to join our celebration.

'We don't know you. How dare you intrude here, where the bravest of the Andartes have gathered to remember the long, bitter, fierce fighting and think of our comrades who were badly injured or killed. Just bugger off to wherever you have been keeping yourself safe.'

As the young man smiled and quietly turned to leave, all heads turned as a clear, young, female voice cried out, 'You fools! You idiots! How dare you offend this young man? Don't you know who he is? I can tell you that his name will for ever be far more famous than your own will ever be! Ladies, Gentlemen, Andartes, I am very proud to introduce you to Charon.'

The roar nearly blew the roof off. Everyone in the bar rushed forward to embrace this single youth whose bravery and daring exploits had been the talk of every *kafenion* and camp from one end of the island to the other. All of them could not wait to kiss him on both cheeks, hug him and slap his back.

After a while, two of the fiercely bearded Kapitäns forced their way through the cheering throng and rescued him. Then the crowd began to chant the name 'Charon' over and over again. He was urged to stand up on a bench and speak to them.

'My dear friends, my fellow Cretans. Thank you from the bottom of my heart for your welcome. How I have dreamt of being amongst you again during my long, lonely, secretive campaign against the German swine. Now my fight is over. It is time for me to try to take up my life again.

'I beg just one thing of you. I am no longer the ferryman of death. Charon has served his purpose well. From now on, please know me as Alexio Petrakis of Galatas, the proud son of Nicolaos and Brigitta, the proud brother of Xanthos, and the proud grandson of Krios and Hestia Petrakis.'

Tom Dunbabin guided him away from the uproarious crowd.

'Well done and well said, Alexio. Now it is time for you to enjoy the very finest of Crete's foods, wines and spirits, then to dance the night away.'

To one side of the bar a group of lads were singing loudly to lively music being played by two old men. The musicians were dressed in the familiar costume of Cretan mountain men. A black laced *sariki* covered their heads. A highly glossed waist-coat and belt with of course a dagger in its sheath. Then baggy brown trousers tucked into black boots specially polished for the occasion. Each sported a magnificent moustache, much loved by Cretans as the very symbol of masculine virility.

One used the three-stringed fiddle known as the *lyra*. This is played with a bow adorned with ribbons. The other played the *santouri*, a very popular stringed instrument.

Just as they began a new tune, with a great yell Alexio leapt up onto the table and with mighty jumps began to dance the Pentosalis. This spirited, lively dance with three basic steps has been danced by Greek men since Minoan times.

Melina sat quietly with her group of excited girlfriends. But her attention had strayed away from them and their chattering. Her gaze was fixed steadily on the young man as he danced.

She knew with total certainty that she had found her man. She knew that they would become husband and wife; that they would have children and hopefully grandchildren; that they would make a new family home in Galatas, which would live again.

Chapter 30

The German Graveyard

1974

It was thirty years from when the occupation ended before Cretans allowed the new Germany to create a military graveyard overlooking Maleme airfield. For all of that time their dead had been hidden away, mainly by priests. The hatred was such that even tractors and steamrollers, used in building and repairing the airfield runways, were destroyed because they were made in Germany. Now it was time to bury their dead in this quiet, peaceful place where their relatives could come and pay their respects.

Alexio Petrakis and his good friend George Psychoundakis rested on their shovels below a cypress tree and watched the opening ceremony. Both often looked back to these terrible days and of the resistance struggle. George was by now better known in the island and across the world as "The Cretan Runner". He had written of his times during the war, in a book bearing that title.

Although just a stripling youth during the war he was very tough and supple. George Psychoundakis thought nothing of running many miles up and down the Lefka Ori mountains under the hot Cretan sun carrying messages between the various resistance groups and the British officers supporting them.

Now the two men spent some of their time looking after the immaculately kept cemetery and the long lines of white crosses. When George was asked by his fellow islanders why he wanted to work there, he would reply, 'I just want to be sure they stay there!'

It was time. The Mayor of Chania introduced a German countess. She had lost all three of her sons who parachuted to their deaths early on in the invasion.

After both had spoken of their wishes that this place would become a haven of peace and reconciliation, a bugler played a sad salute. Then he marched smartly to the foot of the flagpole, untied the lanyard and pulled it firmly. With a soft sound the flag of the new Germany fluttered open in the morning breeze.

The crowd gasped as they saw that another flag had been rolled and concealed within it. Neatly written words on it said:

Never Forget

Bibliography

Crete 1941, Peter D Antill (Osprey)
Crete: The Battle and the Resistance, Antony Beevor (Penguin)
German Aircraft of WW2, Christopher Shepherd (Sidgwick &
     Jackson)
The Cretan Runner, George Psychoundakis (Penguin)
The Lost Battle, Callum MacDonald (MacMillan)
The Mediterranean Fleet (HMSO)
The Rise and Fall of the Third Reich, William Shirer (Redwood)
The Winds of Crete, David MacNeil (Cretan Vista)
Together We Stand, James Holland (Harper & Collins)

The Author

Ian MacMillan, a Glaswegian, spent his career as a Civil and Water Engineer, then as a senior manager mainly in the water industry in Northumbria. After taking early retirement, a period of ill health followed. He, and his wife Jean, then moved to a family home overlooking Gruinard Bay in Wester Ross.

Ian has written poems and short stories for many years. *Charon* is his first novel.

The inspiration for the book came from holidays on the Mediterranean island of Crete when he learnt about the first airborne invasion in history when, in May 1941, the Germans used paratroopers, backed by mountain troops in transport planes, to capture the island from the Allied and Greek defenders.

There was a fiercely fought, extremely close contest before the Nazis gained a sufficient foothold for the Allies to decide to withdraw and again evacuate their war-weary troops, this time to Egypt.

The Cretans, however, had experienced many hostile invasions over the centuries. With support from British Secret

Services they put up a spirited and increasing resistance to the latest, hated occupier.

Since then, Ian has visited the island several times to see battle sites, relevant villages, the countryside, the military graveyards, and the museum and to research the story of the battle, then the resistance struggle and its relevance within World War II.